—THE BLOOD TEXTS—
UNCLE ZEEDIE

For my big sister

Uncle Zeedie is a Fox & Ink Books book

First published in Great Britain in 2025 by
Fox & Ink Books
University of Central Lancashire
Preston, PR1 2HE, UK

Text copyright © Colm Field, 2025
Cover illustration © Keith Robinson, 2025

978-1-916747-75-3

1 3 5 7 9 10 8 6 4 2

The right of Colm Field and Keith Robinson to be identified as the author and illustrator of this work respectively has been asserted in accordance with the Copyright, Designs and Patents Act 1988.

All rights reserved. No part of this publication may be reproduced, stored in a retrieval system, or transmitted in any form or by any means, electronic, mechanical, photocopying, recording or otherwise; or be used to train any AI technologies without the prior permission of the publishers. UCLan Publishing expressly reserves this work from the text and data mining exception subject to EU law.

Set in 10/16pt Kingfisher by Amy Cooper.

A CIP catalogue record for this book is available from the British Library.
Printed and bound in Great Britain by Clays Ltd, Elcograf S.p.A.

THE BLOOD TEXTS
UNCLE ZEEDIE

COLM FIELD

Fox & Ink Books

— Chapter One —

Eight skinny legs scurry across the glass. Eight unblinking eyes study him over dripping fangs. They'll tear his throat, spurt poison into his bloodstream. His mouth will droop and drool, his glassy eyes will roll back as the silk spins, spins, and—

"ARGH! ARGH! ARGH! AR—"

"God, George, calm down!" Lacey shouted. "It's just a spider. Why've you got to be such a wimp?"

"'S'alright, George!" Dad called back. "Just open the window, matey, it'll blow out!" He shot Lacey a frown. "He's alright," he added.

Course he is, Lacey huffed to herself. Three hours they'd been driving through endless countryside, and all the way she'd had to put up with her little brother's panics and demands. *It's too hot. I'm hungry. There's a spider.* No way did she get away with that kinda fuss at twelve.

George opened his window, the wind burst through the car, and with her hair blowing frickin' *everywhere*,

Lacey turned in her seat to show him just how much of a tiresome little snot bubble he was.

Aaaand . . . then she felt bad. George was pinned back into his seat with terror. Staggering along the window towards him, its legs bowing and quivering in the force ten gale, was the dreaded spider.

Lacey sighed. The bug was medium-sized at best. But she wasn't heartless.

"It's still there," she muttered. "*Dad*."

"Oh," her dad said, glancing in the rear-view mirror, "Alright, hang tight, George, there's a shop just ahead."

The car slowed, coming to a halt beside a run-down wooden shack. Lacey took in the withered hanging baskets, the creaking ice cream stand and the sign that read *Rose's Stores* above a dusty, flower-free basket.

"I thought Uncle Zeedie was loaded," she groused. "This place is a dump!" But her dad was already halfway around the car.

"Where is the spider, George?" he asked soothingly.

"It . . . it jumped out the window," George replied lamely, and Lacey couldn't help but grin at the look on her dad's face.

". . . Right-o," he said, trying to sound patient. "Well, now we're here, I'll get us some snacks, then. Your Uncle Zeedie's food was always a bit dodge."

With that latest revelation, their Dad hurried on to the rickety shop. Checking her phone for signal *again,* and finding no bars *again*, Lacey sighed, and got out of the car.

"Dodgy food, crappy shops and no signal," she said, and

slammed the door behind her. "More great reasons to be excited about staying at weirdo not-Uncle Zeedie's house!"

"Mum said not to call him weird," George bleated from the car. "She said Uncle Zeedie's just eccentric."

Lacey ignored him. Uncle Zeedie *was* weird. She hadn't seen him in ages, but she could remember that much. He wasn't really their uncle either, just a friend of their mum and dad's from years before Lacey was born. Before the divorce, Mum and Dad would've spaced out their work, and she and her brother would never have been forced to stay with him out here, in the middle of the Welsh valleys, miles away from her friends, from her girlfriend Mandy.

Before the divorce, she thought, *George could survive a tiny spider crawling across the window.*

"How's the view?" he called to her.

"Get out the car and look yourself," she snapped.

The view was actually incredible. The road ahead plunged like a waterfall, winding into a valley so steep on every side that it might once have been a giant crater. A green delivery van was crawling up the opposite side, tiny against the epic vista. The autumn sun was already ducking behind the hills, dragging a shroud of shadow across the woods below. It made them seem completely wild in a way a townie like Lacey had never seen before; violent mobs of gnarled branches clawing out between dark, suffocating leaves. She took it in, and for some reason she shivered. Then a glint of light caught her attention, and she spotted the big, sprawling, modern mansion sitting in the very middle of it all.

"I hope that's his place, at least," Lacey admitted. "That house is sweet."

"Are you talking about Death House?" a voice said behind her.

George didn't hear the girl approach. He'd been concentrating on two more spiders that were crawling across his window. They were small, even smaller than the last one, and that one had been pretty titchy, if he was to be honest, and so rather than shout out again, he instead sat very still, pretending that they didn't bother him at all. The spiders crawled along the same path the previous spider had taken, scurrying to the top of the glass before tumbling out to the road like it was desperate to get home.

"Bugmakazi," George whispered to himself, and grinned. That was when the girl spoke, making him flinch.

"Are you talking about Death House?"

She looked about the same age as Lacey – fifteen, maybe sixteen – with a tumble of jet-black hair. Her clothes were retro; a pastel-green T-shirt and blue jeans, her skin pale against the faded colours. Straight away George fancied her in that same thoughtless way he fancied most older girls – like she was a popstar or some princess. Which, he'd find out later, she kinda was.

"Death House?" he blurted out. "What do you mean?"

The girl turned, her eyes resting thoughtfully on him as though she was weighing him up.

"It's just a name," she replied, and turned back to face Lacey. "A man lives there, all alone. Do you know him?"

Her Welsh accent was strong. It made her seem older than Lacey somehow. George looked to his sister, and realised with a sinking feeling that she fancied this girl too.

"If it's the right place, he's our Unc— he's called Zeedie," Lacey said. "We're staying with him. Do you live around here?"

The girl smiled, and gestured to the woods down in the valley. "I'm Rose. What's your name?"

"Lacey."

"I'm George," George piped up from the car.

"Are you here for long?" Rose continued, still looking at Lacey, "You should come to our party this evening."

Lacey blinked. George could guess what she was thinking – he was good at that. She was thinking of her girlfriend Mandy back home. She was wondering if it would be cheating just to go to a party with a girl she thought was attractive.

"Sounds good," she said eventually. "So there's more people our age?"

"There's three of us."

"Not a big party, then."

Rose smiled at Lacey. "We've known each other for ever," she said.

Just then, the shop door opened and George's dad walked out, looking confused.

"Hi," he said to Rose. "Do you know who runs that place?

The radio's on, and I called out, but nobody answered."

Rose looked, George thought, strangely surprised to see that anybody had even visited the shop at all.

"It's supposed to be me," she said. "Shoot, sorry!"

"Ah, not to worry, I left your money on the counter," Dad said. He shot a quick, amused glance at Lacey.

"Thanks!" Rose said. She turned to leave, then paused. "So you'll come?" she said to Lacey.

Lacey grinned, and nodded, taking out her phone. "What's your—"

"Phones don't work in the Sink," Rose interrupted, gesturing towards the valley. "Just come to the path around the back of the hedge animals at nine. I'll wait for you there."

"Hedge animals?" George asked. "Uncle Zeedie has *hedge* animals? And what's the Sink?"

Rose smiled, then turned to look at George. "It's all the Sink," she said, and gestured to the valley. "Everything down there."

She had a deep stare, with wide, open eyes that seemed to look right through him. Never the most comfortable talking to girls at the best of times, George swallowed . . . and didn't say any more.

"*Great*," said Lacey, shooting George a look. "I'll see you later, Rose."

Back in the car, Dad handed Lacey the chocolate bars with a wide grin. "How's Mandy?" he asked playfully.

"I don't know," Lacey fired back. "*There's no signal out here to call her.*"

"Touché."

As Dad started the car and pulled back along the road, George looked out of the window back at the shop. Secretly, he hoped Lacey wouldn't go to the party. He didn't want to be left alone the first night here, not in 'Death House', and definitely not if Uncle Zeedie was as weird as Lacey said.

You can't complain, though. Not after the spiders, and the drive, and ... and last week.

Thinking of that awful time in the train station, George gazed unhappily out of the window ...

... and froze.

Beside the shop was a noticeboard, an old one laden down with pamphlets and posters. Even though the font changed on each pamphlet and every poster, George could see two words repeated, again and again:

MISSING CHILD

— Chapter Two —

"Swimming Pool!" Lacey shouted out. "It's got a swimming pool! *Look,* George!"

Uncle Zeedie's house was *massive*, like American houses she'd seen online. All the way up the drive, spotlights illuminated the path ahead. In one direction was a wide tennis court, with tall wire fencing around it. In another was the swimming pool.

"How does Uncle Zeedie own all *this*?" Lacey asked in amazement.

"Not such a bad trip after all, eh?" Dad said with a chuckle. "Zeeds was always very smart. His software company was making megabucks when I was still trying to work out what to do, although weirdly enough I saw something that said the company was in trouble a while ago. Haven't heard anything since, though."

Lacey gazed up at the forest spreading around them. In the distance she caught glimpses of other houses, a roof poking out of the trees here, a chimney poking out there. Lacey wondered which house Rose lived in. Even with those other houses in view, they were so swallowed up by the wild woods that it felt more like some ancient settlement, like they were the first explorers of an untamed land. *With swimming pools and tennis courts*, she corrected herself with a smile.

"Pretty sweet, innit, George?" she said. George didn't answer, didn't even say a word, and Lacey rolled her eyes. He was probably still sore about the stupid spider.

Lacey was wrong, though. George had forgotten all about the spider. What George was thinking about was something he thought of as the Feeling.

He didn't tell people about the Feeling any more, not since all the trouble it had caused at the train station. If he said what it was, they would just tell him he was sad, or worried about his mum and dad. Which he was, but it wasn't that.

The Feeling had begun when they began to descend that winding road down the hill. He'd lied to himself like he always did – *you're just too hot, you're nervous, you're tired* – but the curdling taste had struck the back of his throat like Covid, and as they drove further along his mouth had flooded with saliva like he was gonna puke. Still, he'd tried to pretend that it wasn't what it was, kept urging himself: *don't complain, don't stress Dad out, don't make Lacey look after you*. He'd held his breath, had turned and looked fixedly out of the window so nobody, not even Lacey, would guess what was happening.

But he shouldn't have looked anywhere. He should've shut his eyes until the Feeling passed.

Looking out, George saw this place for real, not what Lacey was wowed into seeing. The square hedges were weed-infested and scruffy, like they'd been hacked at. The lights sparkling on the drive highlighted the dark, muddy stains splotched like sores across it. And yeah, the pool looked amazing . . . but the path beyond it led to those wild, dark woods.

George's eyes followed that path, traced it all the way to the twisted trees. And there, by those trees, stood a boy. A boy who hadn't been there before.

The boy was so far away that George couldn't see his face, although he could see he had a cap on backwards and rips in his denim. Oh, and his mouth. George could see the faceless boy's mouth, because it was opening, wider and wider, until it was stretched out much more wide than a mouth should be, until it was screaming a silent scream that made George want to weep.

And then George had blinked, and the boy had gone.

"Here we are," said Dad. "Zeedie!"

— Chapter Three —

Uncle Zeedie had barely changed. He still had that slightly android face: short, plain, dark hair, no stubble, eyebrows that were almost too perfect, like they'd been crayoned in. In short, he was the basic avatar on every video game, except with bags beneath his eyes. Lacey couldn't remember his eyes looking *that* tired before.

"Zeeds," Dad said happily. "How's it going, mate?"

"Well– I– I'm well, Daniel," Uncle Zeedie said awkwardly, and smeared a sheen of sweat across his forehead with the back of his hand. "How are you? I trust the drive was not too long?"

"Not at all. This place is amazing, Zeeds!"

"Yes?" Uncle Zeedie said. "Good." He sounded surprised by the compliment, Lacey thought.

"Hey, Uncle Zeedie," she said with a smile. She didn't hug him. It was one of those things they knew, something her parents had always drilled in. *Don't hug Uncle Zeeds. Don't even shake hands. He doesn't like to be touched.*

"Larissa," Uncle Zeedie said. She *hated* that name. "How are you? Your father tells me you enjoy reading."

"I . . . yeah, I guess." Lacey did read, it just wasn't the first thing she'd say about herself. *Urgh*, this was even more uncomfortable than she'd expected. Uncle Zeedie was odder than she remembered; his brow constantly sweating, a smile on his face that looked not just forced, but scratched in with a rusty blade.

Her dad, to be fair, read the awks and stepped in.

"Hey, Zeeds, thanks for having the kids, especially at such short notice. I'd rang *everybody*, it was just . . ."

"So you called a number of people," Uncle Zeedie said.

Too late, Lacey's dad realised what he'd said. *I called everyone before I called you.*

"I–it's a massive help," he continued, reddening. "Becky's not giving an inch, mate, she's a flipping nightmare, like just *grow up*, she—"

Dad broke off with a glance to Lacey, but she'd already looked away, stomach curdling. Mum and Dad had broken up almost a year ago, and it hadn't exactly been a love story before . . . but lately things were horrible between them. They hardly ever spoke, and every chance they got they would badmouth one another, before breaking off and glancing at her with this *'I can't say too much'* BS.

Lacey didn't blame her dad for having to work this weekend, and didn't blame her mum for having to work either. It was the comment that hurt, the shots fired. They were blasting away at each other, and Lacey kept getting clipped.

And, because she *was* a good big sister, her next worry was that George had taken a bullet as well. She looked to see if he'd heard . . . and realised that George was still in the car.

"Is George okay?" Uncle Zeedie asked.

George's door was open, but he'd shuffled over to the other side. Lacey couldn't see his face but his body looked petrified, completely frozen. He was staring out of the window, out to the swimming pool.

"George?" said Dad. "C'mon, Georgie, out ya get, mate."

Still no movement. Uncle Zeedie looked at them both, then just as Lacey sighed and began, "I'll get him—"

"I can do it," Uncle Zeedie cut in, with a friendship that to Lacey's ears sounded false. Awkwardly, he moved around the car, pulled at the door handle and . . .

George tumbled through the opening door and out of the car. Even worse, he didn't try to regain his balance, but threw his arms around Uncle Zeedie and clutched to him in a tight toddler's hug.

"—ck's sakes," Dad muttered.

". . . Ugh," Uncle Zeedie said. He didn't close his arms around George, just stood there, hands splayed out like they should be webbed. Lacey watched with a mixture of horror and fascination. It wasn't like the movies, where the adorable kid melts the man's heart. It was dreadful. George looked like he was losing his mind; Zeedie looked nauseous.

"Okay, George," Dad said. "Let go now. George. George!"

George let go and Uncle Zeedie staggered back slightly, that look of disgust still on his face. Dad smiled his embarrassed smile, his *'There'd be hell to pay if you weren't here'* smile.

"We'll get the bags in, won't we, George!" he said jovially.

"Good," said Zeedie. He walked straight inside, not waiting, not offering "No, no, let me carry them." He just walked in, brushing fiercely at his clothes where George had hugged him, as though trying to wipe some terrible stain away.

"Didn't protest much, did he?!" Lacey joked. But Dad was already leaning in to mutter angrily to George.

"You are *too* old for this behaviour."

And, for the first time all day, Lacey felt like her brother had been given a raw deal.

Chapter Four

Lacey had to admit it, this house was *amazing*. She walked through the front door into a cavernous, open-plan living room, lined on one side with huge windows that let in all the daylight from outside. A wide, double door led to a spacious kitchen with granite tops. A floating staircase ran along the wall in front of her, and far beyond that she could see the back door leading to what looked like the hedge animals.

(There was also a door beneath the floating stairs. George paused before it, and then swiftly walked past. But Lacey didn't think much about this until later.)

"Thanks again for this, Zeeds, I'd told Becky about this conference *months* ago, but she makes out like I didn't because *she* didn't put it in the calendar..."

Their dad followed Uncle Zeedie into the kitchen, and not wanting to hear any more, Lacey took a look upstairs, George behind her. The room right by the stairs with a suit jacket hanging on the door was clearly Uncle Zeedie's, and as they reached the next room along, she gestured at it, glancing back to her brother.

"That's your room, George," she said firmly. Hell no did she wanna be stuck next door to Uncle Zeedie if she was sneaking out to meet Rose.

"Okay," George said moodily, and went into 'his' room. Keen to get some space away from both her brother and Uncle Zeedie, Lacey looked around for anywhere further away. But there was only one more bedroom around the other side, and a doorway with nothing but...

"That's more like it," Lacey said out loud, as the door swung open to reveal a spiral staircase leading up to more bedrooms. She climbed up them, hoping to get a room as isolated as possible... but when she got up there, the rooms were all bare, no mattresses, no carpet, even, as if they'd been stripped clean. Only one room had furniture, and that looked like Uncle Zeedie's office.

"Well I don't wanna be next to that anyway," she grumbled, and went back downstairs.

It wouldn't be so bad. The first-floor landing was basically a balcony that looked over the massive ground floor below. Walking all the way around it, looking down at the huge living room and the fantastic swimming pool through those wall-to-wall windows, Lacey felt her mood lift. Then she went into the last bedroom, and grinned.

"These bedrooms are massive, George!" she shouted. "King-size beds! George, have you got a king-size bed? And a..."

She broke off, looking across the large, carpeted bedroom in disbelief, before striding to the door in the opposite corner.

"Our own bathrooms! George, have you got your own bathroom? *George!*" With an excited laugh at the huge, deluxe en-suite bathroom, Lacey hurried back through her bedroom, back out to the landing...

... And came to an abrupt halt.

"What is it?"

George was standing in his bedroom door. He wore that low-browed scowl she dreaded, the one he always wore when he was scared and expecting her to tell him off.

"What's wrong?"

"S'a bit freaky," he muttered.

"George, it's a massive bedroom," she sighed. "There's, like, *marble* in the bathroom."

George shrugged. A needle of annoyance dug into Lacey's brain.

"It's not freaky," she demanded. "And – you've been saying everything's freaky lately. I don't wanna bring up the train station, but—"

"I was right about that train station."

"What do you even mean *right*, you—"

"I know it seems crazy, but I was right. I looked it up and—"

"*George,* STOP!"

George flinched, shocked by her sudden anger.

"George, you freaked out. Dad had to drive up and carry you out of there. That's not..."

"... Normal," George said, hurt in his eyes.

Lacey breathed out, and tried again.

"George, this is a really cool place. You know how rubbish it's been at home. Uncle Zeedie is . . . okay, so he's flipping *strange*, but . . . this house is really cool, and there's a pool and I want to hang out with Rose and . . . I really need this."

She *hated* the catch in her voice. It made her angry, not so much at George as at Mum and Dad, at their horrible situation. Finally George nodded, and as he turned away, looking sadder than ever, Lacey felt a painful sense of guilt.

"*Bunny Versus Monkey* tonight?" she blurted out.

George paused. He turned.

"Yes, please," he said, and his wide, grateful smile made Lacey feel like he'd stitched her *right* up.

— Chapter Five —

"So, tuna mayonnaise is nice . . . but with sweetcorn isn't?"

George smiled, and shook his head at Uncle Zeedie.

"Nope. And definitely not with butter. Butter's disgusting."

After a guilty, hurried goodbye, their dad had left, and night was racing into the steep valley. They'd spent the last hour exploring the house, which was, like outside, very grand but . . . actually kinda faded. A surprising number of rooms were plain white, with no furniture in at all, making the place feel cold. The only things that George had particularly liked were the loft and the loft blinds.

They hadn't seen the loft at first. It was just a closed hatch in the ceiling of the second floor, a blue cord hanging from it. George, who never saw a button he didn't want to press, pulled hard at the cord – and was nearly knocked out by the ladder that tumbled down. Lacey had had a go at him, but when they climbed up she'd been impressed. The loft was small, but every side of it was a window.

"That's why the roof was glinting when I saw the house earlier!" Lacey said. "How do we open these blinds?"

George had already found the clicker, a small plastic box like a television remote. He pressed the up arrow . . . and as the blinds rolled up with a whirr, the dying sunlight shone through the windows, illuminating an epic view of the sprawling woods all around them. It was like something from Tolkien, and for a moment George forgot the Feeling completely. He liked this loft, and the blinds, very much.

Then Uncle Zeedie had called them down for some food.

"Okay then, tuna mayonnaise on bread it is," Uncle Zeedie said now, and gave a pale smile. Everything about him was pale. "*Order received*," he added in a robotic voice.

Ouch, George thought, *I'm a geek and even I don't get why you did that.* He gave a polite smile back, the kind you give for crap jokes, looked around the kitchen and tried to figure out why it looked so tired. The kitchen tops were big and shiny, but the shine was grubby and fading. The windows were surprisingly small and made the room quite dark. Worst of all was the sour smell of rotten milk that you only *just* noticed when you breathed in. George was looking for what might be causing it, when he noticed something.

"What did you do to your hand?" he asked Uncle Zeedie.

Uncle Zeedie didn't reply for a long moment. The knuckles of his hand, which held the bread knife, were deeply bruised, as though he'd been punching something *hard*.

"I caught it on something."

George nodded, and glanced to Lacey, wondering what

she would say to this odd excuse. But she was swiping at her phone, holding it up, then frowning.

"The signal here's really bad, Uncle Zeedie."

"True," Zeedie admitted. "You have to go to the top of the hill to get any, and even then it comes and goes. I normally rely on the Wi-Fi, but that's out as well."

"Wait..." said Lacey, looking alarmed. "There's no Wi-Fi? So... there's no phones, *at all?*"

"Not right now, sorry," said Zeedie. He didn't sound sorry, George thought.

Lacey stared at Uncle Zeedie in disbelief. After a moment she made an exasperated noise.

"Great," she said, and left, shaking her head.

Uncle Zeedie stared as she left. Then, as if coming out of a trance, he blinked, and looked back at George.

"Your sandwich," he said, and handed over the plate. "If you don't mind, I'm going to bed. I'm quite tired. I was up late working last night."

"Er, okay. Thanks for the sandwich, Uncle Zeedie."

George had always been good at telling what people were thinking. Since Mum and Dad's divorce, it had been heightened into what felt like a sixth sense. And now, as Uncle Zeedie's footsteps climbed the stairs, he had the strangest feeling that he was terrified of somehow being found out.

But found out for what? George thought. He took a bite from the sandwich, caught a glimpse of the bottom and...

George threw the sandwich back down, stumbling off the bar stool in shock. He reached out, flipped the sandwich over, and retched, till his eyes watered and a gulp of air escaped from his pulsing throat.

The bottom slice of bread was green, crusted over with a furry mould.

Chapter Six

"Urgh," said Lacey, frowning at the sandwich. "He gave you this?"

"You were there!" George protested. "You saw him make the sandwich!"

"Yeah, I believe you, s'just . . ." Lacey broke off, staring at the mouldy bread. She shuddered, took the plate, and tipped the sandwich into the bin. "I'll make you another one."

"Is Uncle Zeedie . . . like you remember him?" George asked.

"Well . . . I remembered him being odd before," Lacey admitted. George thought about this, staring into the distance before turning his green eyes back to her.

"He's lying to us," he announced.

"What? What about?"

". . . I don't know."

For a moment, Lacey glared, and George regretted saying so much. He'd made things difficult lately, he knew he had. Memories of the train station flashed through his mind, of terror, then of horrible, horrible embarrassment. But then Lacey frowned.

"I thought Uncle Zeedie ran a big successful business? If there's no Wi-Fi and no phone signal, then how was he up late doing work?"

———

Several hours later, Lacey sat back and finished the page.

"And... that's all I'm reading tonight."

"Oh no, no, come on, please, just a bit more, *please!*" George cried.

She sighed, and checked her phone. Nearly 9pm and *still* no bars. She had to be at the old treehouse to meet Rose, and she had no way of telling her she would be late. Matter of fact, she couldn't even contact Rose if she got the signal. With an inward groan, Lacey looked between the gap in the curtains at the rustling trees outside, and cursed. How could she be so stupid, not even to get a number, a profile, nothing?

"One more?" George said hopefully behind her.

"Do you know how many sisters read to their *twelve-year-old brother?*" she snapped. "Especially a comic book!" But she sat down. George was scared, and right now, with every wall lit perfectly and bare, Lacey could see why. It was smart this place, but there was no soul to it, none at all. Back home their walls seemed to let in every noise from every side, every TV in every nearby room, every car outside. But here all the sound seemed swallowed up by the walls. Until one escaped from the void.

Crick...

It was barely there, but Lacey heard it. Curious, she went to the door and looked out to the landing. There was nobody there. But the door to Uncle Zeedie's room was being softly closed.

She grimaced. He *was* odd, Uncle Zeedie. He was *off*.

"Lacey?" George sounded fragile. "Lace, what is it?"

"Nothing," Lacey said, and opened the door to show him. "See? Alright, so ten more minutes?"

— Chapter Seven —

The security lights round the back of the house didn't work. The moon had disappeared behind the wooded hillside ahead. Only her torchlight cut between the gnarled hedge plants, shining up the mulch path that led into the thickened woods, before it was swamped by darkness.

"Rose?" Lacey called out nervously. She turned and took in the house, silent and brooding behind her. As modern as it was, it somehow became more sinister the more she looked at it. Lacey felt a sudden pang of guilt for leaving George alone here . . . but no. No. How many older siblings read their kid brother to sleep? How many times had she wished for that bit of freedom, freedom from worrying about him all the time? This was that break, and she deserved it.

Her mouth set, she strode quietly up the hill. Was this the right path? Rose had said the one "*behind the hedge animals*". It had to be here; a garden straight out of a stately manor home, small green hedges dotted about left and right among the overgrown grasses. But none of these hedges resembled animals that Lacey had ever seen.

At least not until she passed them by. Trudging up the steep path until she reached the opening between the trees, Lacey looked back downhill, and paused. They *were* hedge animals, she could see from up here – or at least they once were. Topiary it was called, wasn't it? When you pruned plants into careful shapes and even into figures, like carved statues of animals. But these topiary animals hadn't been cared for for a long time.

Their figures were twisted almost beyond recognition, their leaves overgrown and springing out in every direction. One hedge had the alert ears of a hare; ears that disappeared into a chaotic curled-up bush, as though the hare was curled up in fright. Another used to be a stag, Lacey could see, but it looked rabid, its green antlers drooping and twisted. Together these hedge animals leaned up the hill toward Lacey, as though they were kneeling before her, and as she felt the pitch-black woods swallowing the air behind her, a thin slither of fear crept up between her shoulder blades.

She'd made a mistake coming here.

SNAP

Lacey whirled around, breathing hard.

"Rose?" she said again. But her voice carried no further than the torchlight. Like the hedge animals, the path into the woods was overgrown, tree branches draped like limbs across every side. The air was absolutely still, and yet Lacey was sure she'd heard something – a twig, a branch . . . something.

"Probably a fox," she said out loud. But she didn't want to be here any more. Forget meeting Rose, Lacey had a girlfriend anyway, and—

SNAP

That had come from the hedge animals themselves. Lacey spun back around, her torchlight dancing across the tortured topiary beasts. Forget *this*, she thought angrily. She walked back down the path and . . .

SNAP

The shape emerged in slow motion, out from the woods behind her. Lacey spun her torch around, arms flailing, and tripped, falling down the hill. She hit the ground hard and slid, the breath punched out of her, her heartbeat petrified. The figure loomed towards her, and there was nothing she could do to stop it.

"Lacey?" Rose said. "Are you okay? I'm sorry, I didn't mean to scare you. Are you okay?!"

"Yes," Lacey said. She began to laugh, just glad that Rose couldn't see how red her face had gone.

— Chapter Eight —

George slept fitfully. His dreams were troubled, with arguments and anger and the threat of violence just on the edge of the fog. It was as if, being asleep, he was being more honest. And sleeping George knew, sleeping George didn't pretend: death was all around them, and both he and Lacey were in terrible danger.

"WAKE UP!" sleeping George screamed. *"WAKE UP AND RUN FOR YOUR LIVES!"*

But George didn't wake up. Echoes of his sister's bored reading voice kept him safe in the sleeping fog, memories of bright, funny cartoons making that fog thicker still. Then, just as George was finally at rest, the fog began to clear, and the shrieks of his sleeping self pierced through.

"WAKE UP! WAKE UP, GEORGE, WAKE U—"

George awoke. Just his bedside lamp was on, a small glowing corner around him, and a wide area of darkness around that. He closed his eyes and squirmed under the toasty duvet . . . only to get that sharp, annoying feeling. He needed the toilet. He turned on his elbow and pushed himself up, grunting to the shape in the armchair.

"You did stay! Thanks, Lacey."

There was no reply. His sister must've fallen asleep too. George owed her for this. They fought a lot, and sometimes she could be mean, but she was there for him when it counted.

Sighing, he dropped out of bed and padded across the floor. The carpet was so thick and warm, not like his worn old solar system rug at home. Approaching the darkened bathroom, George felt a familiar fear build up inside, but dim lamps switched on automatically as he reached the door, putting his mind at ease.

"George?"

George heard it, and turned back to his sister . . .

But there was nobody in the armchair at all.

— Chapter Nine —

"So this is Kendra," said Rose.

"Hey, Kendra!" said Lacey with a smile. The tall, pale girl gave Lacey a wave and a slightly wild laugh.

They had walked a short way up a winding path that darkness had made a maze. Lacey had talked most of the way, which she did when she was nervous, but when she glanced at Rose the other girl had looked happy to listen. Soon the trees had opened up, into a clearing that was lit by camping lanterns of all shapes and sizes. In a rough circle round the middle were six tall rocks. Inside that circle were six smaller rocks, smoothed into stools. Rose's friends were sat on two of these stools, which, okay, made Lacey feel like she was on display, but at least Kendra seemed friendly. Unlike the brooding, angry boy sat moodily next to her.

"This is River," Rose said.

"Er, hi," said Lacey, and felt the smile slip from her face. River glowered at her ... and didn't reply.

"*River*," Rose said.

"Hi," River said at last, but his voice was almost completely flat. Wondering what she'd done wrong, Lacey glanced at Rose, who shrugged sympathetically.

"This place is amazing!" Lacey said, trying to make conversation. "How did you guys find it?"

"We know *everywhere* here," Kendra said confidentially, then grinned. "It's nice, isn't it? It used to be better, before the—"

"Kendra." River said it harshly, as if she were about to mention a forbidden secret.

"Uhhh, *okay*," Lacey said. "So you guys don't like to share the goss about . . . what's this place called?"

Her eyes rested on a crumbling wooden sign beside a vine-strewn rock. The sign looked ancient and decayed, its edges jagged. Carved into it, in an ornate script that was almost too perfect to have been done by hand, were two words:

ega

ivin

"Ega ivin," Lacey read aloud. "What does that mean, then?"

Again, nobody answered, although River made a scoffing sound. Lacey, who wasn't one for secrets, was about to say that she was getting a bit fed up with this rude arsehole, and why did they invite her if they weren't going to say anything, when River looked back at her and said something that took her aback.

"You're in Death House," he said simply.

"River!" Rose warned.

"Death House?" Lacey repeated, feeling alarmed.

"It's only a name," Rose repeated. But River stared keenly at her, at Kendra, then at Lacey.

"Rose?"

Smirking, River took a set of crumpled pamphlets out of his pocket and handed them over. On them all was the same message.

MISSING CHILD

"What . . ." Lacey said, going through them. There was a boy with a black hoodie and bad acne. There was a girl with a retainer, another girl with braids in her hair. Another boy with—

"They . . . they all went missing nearby?" Lacey said slowly. Rose didn't answer. Was she annoyed at River for sharing these? Lacey couldn't tell. A cold, clammy feeling was settling over her.

"And you think this has something to do with . . ." She couldn't even say it.

River did.

"Your Uncle Zeedie lives at Death House."

"He's not my real uncle," Lacey retorted quickly, and part of her felt guilty for saying that. "He's just a friend of my parents. I've barely seen him for years. We're only here because . . ." Eventually, she waved it away. "Anyway, I'm not defending him or myself to *you* unless you tell me what's going on."

She stared stonily at the others, who stared back. She'd surprised them, she knew. Lacey had had years of dealing with rows between her parents. She wanted to get along with this gang. But she wasn't going to sell herself short, *especially* not if they were being unfriendly.

"She's right," Rose said to River. "You should say sorry."

River stared. His lip curled and he looked away, muttering something in Welsh that Lacey couldn't understand. It sounded like *cig noeth*.

"River," said Rose, sharply.

"Sorry," he said at last.

"So what are you saying, you think these kids are missing because of Zeedie?" Lacey asked incredulously . . . "Because that's just . . . he's not . . . it must be someone else around here."

"There's nobody else here," Kendra said. She, at least, sounded sympathetic.

"I . . ." Lacey began, then trailed off. Her three new friends – *were they friends?* – looked at one another. They didn't seem mean. If anything they seemed sorry for her, which was worse.

"I haven't even seen him in years," she added in a small voice.

Rose stepped forwards and held out her hand.

"I'm sorry, Lacey," she said. "Do you want to come and look over the Sink?"

"Changing the subject, just like that?" Lacey said, surprised. But still, she took the offered hand. Rose's fingers were icy, and touching them sent a swirl of guilty thoughts about her girlfriend Mandy back home. Weirdly enough it was nice to feel the guilt and confusion. Anything to drown out the same horrible question echoing through her mind repeatedly.

Could Uncle Zeedie really have something to do with the missing children?

After the comfort of the lantern-lit clearing, the path through thick woods seemed wilder than ever. Lacey was in shape, was even trying for her local swimming team, but she was soon out of breath. Rose, on the other hand, barely broke her stride. Lacey was just about to give in and beg her to slow down . . . when the trees cleared once again. This time the moon blared in, a high and cold beam of light that bathed the entire valley in blue. With Rose standing beside her, Lacey took a breath at the beauty below.

"I still don't get how you go without phones all the time," Lacey admitted, "But it is kinda amazing here."

"It's paradise," Rose said with a smile. Her eyes met Lacey's, and seemed to grow larger.

Lacey smiled back. "And I still don't know anything about you guys. Where's your house, even?"

"Look." She took Lacey by the arm, and pointed it down the hill to where a darkened house poked out between the trees. The house wasn't too far from Uncle Zeedie's, just a short way on the other side of the valley.

"Don't your parents mind you going out this late?"

Rose paused. Then she shook her head.

"They don't care," she said. Sadder words than she made

them sound. Lacey thought of all the times she'd pretended not to be fazed by her parents' divorce, and felt a pang of empathy.

"Look . . ." she began. But Rose was looking curiously along the valley, down at Uncle Zeedie's house.

"Someone's there," she said, and pointed.

Lacey squinted, and saw what Rose meant.

"God, your eyes are *good*," she admitted. But Rose was right. There was someone dragging something heavy, just near the back fence. They were struggling with it, but they managed to haul it all the way round the side of the house, out of view.

Lacey turned to see Rose looking at her, a quizzical smile on her face. The air was quiet, almost still. Somewhere in her mind Mandy was glaring at her, but from a distance. Lacey opened her mouth to speak . . .

And a scream filled the air.

"What was that?" Rose exclaimed, but Lacey was already looking down the valley.

"George," she said, and ran.

— Chapter Ten —

George stood in the bathroom doorway, staring at the empty armchair, his mouth turned down. There *had* been something there, he was sure of it. He wanted to call out, but part of him knew there would be trouble for Lacey if he did. She'd gone out, for sure. And...

And honestly, he was a bit freaked out to call out for Uncle Zeedie. He seemed ... changed, like he was missing something from the last time George met him. So no, George had to toughen up a bit, stop being a baby.

Calming down reminded George that he needed to pee. It came suddenly, and he hurried on into the dark bathroom, only just reaching the toilet in time. The tiles felt warm beneath his toes, a nice comfort that helped him relax even more, and by the time George flushed the toilet he was looking straight into the mirrored wall above it without worrying that some monster would jump out at him. He felt proud, facing up to his fears. He'd tell Lacey in the morning, and she'd be impressed.

George went and washed his hands, glancing only twice

in the mirror to where the empty armchair sat next to his bed. It was fine – he'd put on his podcast and fall asleep. It was fine. He switched off the tap and dried his hands, as the water gurgled down the drain, and then ...

Plink.

George looked back at the sink. It sounded like something had dropped far, like the last drop from a tap into a deep, deep well. He looked closer, and ...

A scratching sound was coming up the plughole.

Suddenly George felt a chill between his toes, as though the marble had grown cold. His throat went dry, and the cold spread – up his legs, across his bare back. Again the sound came from the sink, and with the Feeling drawing his gaze like a blood-spattered car crash, George leaned forwards to stare closer, closer at the small, grilled plughole, until his eyeball was just centimetres above it. There were water drops. There was darkness.

Then abruptly, pushed up the pipe till it struck the grill, there was peach skin, bright-blue eyes and neon-pink lips. It was a Barbie doll, and as it's mildew-slimed face pressed up against the metal, a girl's urgent whisper drifted out with it.

"*We're down here, George. Deep down, as far as you can go.*"

George screamed. Then he screamed again, and again, stumbling out to the bedroom.

"Lacey! Uncle Zeedie, Uncle Zeedie, HELP!"

The response was swift – noises downstairs, a door opening, footsteps running to the staircase.

"Children?" Zeedie called. "George?"

George froze at the top of the stairs and didn't move, his eyes shut tight. A cold finger touched the back of his hand and he jerked away.

"NO!" he begged.

"George," Zeedie said, and at last George opened his eyes. Zeedie was several stairs below him, his face masked by shadow. "George? Did you have a bad dream?"

Why is his voice so flat? Why doesn't he hug, why—

"I want Lacey," George said, trying desperately not to blub. "Where is she?" He'd given away that she wasn't in the house just like he hadn't wanted to, but he didn't care any more.

Zeedie looked along the balcony to Lacey's open bedroom door, confusion on his face. Then his expression tightened.

"She went out," George said.

It could not have been timed any worse. Downstairs, the back door clattered open, and Lacey rushed across the hallway towards the stairs.

"George!" she whispered . . . then stopped before the balcony, looking guiltily up at Uncle Zeedie as she pulled down her snood. Seeing the tight-lipped displeasure on his face, George felt another pang of guilt at having dobbed Lacey in. Still, he couldn't help but notice something.

"Why are you all muddy?" he said to Zeedie. But Uncle Zeedie didn't answer the question.

—Chapter Eleven—

"You know, if I were to treat you with the respect of an adult," Uncle Zeedie said coldly, "I would ask that if you genuinely did not see anything wrong with your going out so late, then why did you go to such effort to keep it a secret?"

Lacey sighed. This was doing her head in. Why was he making it such a big deal?

"I didn't keep it secret," she lied.

"Clearly you did not tell me."

"*Clearly that is true.*" Lacey copied him before she could stop herself, imitating his geeky, slightly robotic voice. Zeedie's face froze, and at once she regretted being so petty. She supped her juice and looked away.

The morning was cold, and the kitchen was dark. Still, she'd brought her swimming kit down that morning, was going to have a dip in the pool. It was more than she'd get to do back home.

"Sorry," she said. He didn't react, and she repeated it more loudly. "Sorry, Uncle Zeedie."

He blinked and looked up, as though he'd been brooding

on something more than just her sneaking out. "Right," he said.

"Er, I think George is okay, by the way. I heard him moving around up there. I think he's probably just embarrassed."

"Right."

Lacey's concern was growing. Uncle Zeedie wasn't right – like *really* not right. As tired as he'd looked yesterday, the bags beneath his eyes could've carried shopping today. There was an unpleasant odour of sour milk. She almost asked Uncle Zeedie about it, but he'd downed his coffee, was taking out some bread to toast and . . .

"Oh, you might want to check that bread is okay," Lacey said.

Confused, Zeedie looked at the bread, then, looking at her strangely, took two pieces out.

"It is fine," he said, "I have this bread delivered fresh."

"Oh, it . . . The sandwich you made George yesterday? The bottom slice had loads of mould on it. I mean, like, *loads* of mould."

Uncle Zeedie looked through the loaf. He shook his head. "These are all okay."

"Yeah, I can see that . . ." Lacey trailed off, frustrated. "It was *fuzzy*."

"The fuzzy mould we see on bread are colonies of spores. When anything decays, these spores travel through the air inside the package and grow on other parts of the bread. It would not simply gather on one piece of bread alone."

Lacey stared at him. Was he suggesting she'd made it up?

Why would she even *do* that?

"I'm going swimming," she said at last. Uncle Zeedie didn't reply, as she got up and left the kitchen. She picked up her swimming bag in the hallway and was about to go outside, when she paused, noticing the door beneath the floating staircase again. They'd never looked in it yesterday.

"Where's this door go?" she called back. He took so long to answer she almost wondered if he'd completely zoned out.

"It is allegedly a basement. But it is inaccessible. The door is locked and I have not yet located the key."

"Okaaay," Lacey said. As quietly as she could, she reached out and tried the handle. It wouldn't turn, like Uncle Zeedie had said. But still she knew he was lying.

There, just beneath the handle, was a sharp, fresh scratch… and a small red stain.

Suddenly she didn't want to be on her own.

———

After a morning of hiding away from both Lacey and Zeedie, George got changed. The light was on in the bathroom, and everything was clean and clear, no sign of anything he'd seen the night before. He wondered if he was losing his mind. Part of him wanted to sleep, but he didn't want to be too awake later.

George had always been sensitive. Not in a weepy way, like his mum and dad said he was; more like he'd always felt the presence of another life out there, the murmurs of a world just beneath the one people could see and touch. (And okay, also in a bit of a weepy way.)

But the break-up? That had been such an earth-shattering event, it was like *life* had been ripped open – not so much George himself, but everything else. Suddenly he could see all the *deep* scars, could tell when people were lying, or secretly angry, or devastatingly sad. Things had been getting worse, and when he'd flipped out in the train station last week, his mum – who'd always made aggy jokes about her posh friend's therapist – had asked, "Would you like to talk to someone about this, George?"

No way. Not to anyone.

It had come out of nowhere. Their mum was taking them to their dad's, and because her car was in the garage they were taking the train. Mum had been on the phone to one of her friends, and George had been sitting happily reading his gaming book, when he'd noticed Lacey scowling.

"What?" he'd mouthed to her, but Lacey had flinched, then shook her head and looked away.

That was when George tuned in to his mum's conversation.

"And as you can imagine, you-know-who was being a whiny little s-o-b about the whole thing, like he's the only one who works for a living," she was saying, "Because it's not like he's even a success, anyway. I know. Yeah, exactly!"

George had frowned. Mum was talking about Dad. And while her tone was friendly, her words weren't.

"Caught him speaking to the dental nurse that time. I mean, like come on, you preposterous man, have you taken a look

at yourself lately? Maybe try for her grandma, you might have more chance!"

Suddenly George had felt awfully tired. His throat had dried out, and the palms of his hands had been sweaty and cold. He'd got up, which was a mistake as the platform had begun to list like a ship on stormy waters, and as Lacey said "You alright?" sounding underwater, George had looked past her to the station clock.

Hanging beneath it were five bodies. Their insides were outside.

"Do . . . do . . . do you see them?" His voice was hoarse. And before she could answer, he'd begun to scream . . .

George took a sharp breath, and fell back into the present. It was all okay. He was back on this comfy bed in Uncle Zeedie's house. There was nothing unnatural around him – at least not right now. He should stop doing it, should stop thinking about the station, and ghosts, and visions of hanging bodies. He *would* stop thinking about it, and if his mum *did* send him to a therapist, he wouldn't tell the therapist anything about it.

Not even what he found out about those hanging bodies he saw . . .

And George was just about to trouble over *that* thought, when his sister appeared in the door.

"Safe safe, smellface," she said. "Wanna go to the pool?"

—Chapter Twelve—

The swimming pool was a complete change from the small overcrowded squares of wee George always dreaded on their usual holidays. It was massive, and deep, the water just warm enough in the sweet fresh air. Lacey had a swimming gala coming up, and so George helped her train, racing her and *almost* keeping up at first. By the time he was too exhausted to swim any more, he leaned back and floated, and forgot all about his visions, forgot about ever being scared at all.

"George," Lacey's voice echoed through the water, and he sat up. "Is that Uncle Zeedie?"

George looked up, and paused. It was hard to see him at first, there at the very top of the building, up in the small, windowed loft. But there he was, Uncle Zeedie, staring out at the valley. After a moment, the loft blinds began to roll smoothly down, hiding Uncle Zeedie behind them.

"You know when we first got here, and you . . . hugged him?" Lacey asked.

George felt his face grow warm. "Yep," he said shortly.

"So . . . why did you do that?"

George considered his response. If he was going to tell anyone, it would be Lacey. But . . .

"Uh-uh," he said at last, shaking his head. "Not telling."

Lacey considered this, then shrugged.

"Fairy nuff," she said at last. Then she leaned in and muttered, "I don't care what Dad says, though. That guy's gone frickin' *weird*. He was out here last night, you know. He was dragging something, but I couldn't see what it was. And that door in the main room, the one under the stairs? He said he's never been down there, but there's a scratch on it, dirt on the floor and blood on the handle."

"*Blood?*"

Lacey nodded.

"I'm telling ya. Guy's weird."

George didn't know what to think. He thought of himself as 'weird'. *Especially after the train station.* But the mouldy sandwich, the mysteriously locked door? And the voice from last night?

We're all down here, George . . .

"And you know that Rose?" Lacey continued. "I met up with her and her friends last night. And she said . . ."

George waited. But Lacey had hesitated.

"What?"

". . . Nah, s'not fair on him," Lacey decided. "Anyway, I don't want you having nightmares and embarrassing yourself again."

George chuckled. She had a way, Lacey, of making harsh

jokes not that harsh.

"I'm getting out," he said at last, and before she could speak, he splashed water into her face.

"Youuuu . . ." Lacey roared, and lunged towards him. Giggling, George pulled himself out of the pool as quickly as he could and scampered to the changing rooms.

When he glanced back up at the loft, the blinds were completely shut.

The changing rooms would've been nice, once. Now, though, they felt dark and dank; low, cramped ceilings and cold tiled floors that felt dirty on George's wet feet. Except for the wooden lockers, everything was white, but again this just highlighted the decay; the cracked tiles, the yellow patches on the ceiling, the bubbled and blistered paintwork. Even the locks on those sleek wooden lockers were rusted shut.

George couldn't get out of here fast enough; barely drying himself before throwing his T-shirt on, even though it clung uncomfortably to his still-wet back. At one point he spotted a cluster of cobwebs in the ceiling corner, and scoured the room for the massive spider that made them. But there was nothing.

He was just pulling his socks on when he heard it: a sound ahead. It was a tap, barely anything, from inside those rusted-up lockers.

Then . . . silence.

A chill glanced his spine, the changing rooms now

darker than before. George squeezed his trainers on without undoing them, the heel folding up as he got to his feet. He wanted to run, but didn't. His dad's voice echoed through his mind.

You are TOO old for this behaviour.

"Sack it," he said, turning away from the noise, and as he gathered his stuff he whistled as loudly as he could.

Have you ever done this? Have you ever been scared and unable to do anything about it but act the fool? That's what George did then. His whistle grew hoarse so he sang, belting out pop songs in a silly voice. He didn't just pack his swimming bag, he *punched* his flippin' clothes in, pulled the drawstring tight and swung it over his shoulder, and faced the . . .

—A locker door was swinging open.

Not fast, not at all; it was more like it had been gently prodded open from the inside. The door opened about halfway, letting out a quiet creak as it came to a halt, the space behind it shrouded in black. It was the last locker on the row, the one by the exit.

George stared at it. He felt an icy band around his forearm, looked down and realised it was his own hand, grabbing in fear and squeezing tight. He struggled to breathe. The air felt mouldy, like it was infecting his lungs.

"Sack it," he choked out, "SACK IT."

And George *strode*, marching forwards and singing and whistling, swinging his swimming bag in time. Ten steps it was, to pass that open locker and reach the exit, and even though terror was squeezing his guts in clammy hands, even though his only thought was *'Don't look at the locker, don't look at the locker'*, he didn't speed up. Not until he swung the bag too hard around, smacked it into the locker door and...

He didn't mean to turn around. He'd done so well, ignoring the dark void inside the locker. But something glinted in that darkness. Something small, no bigger than a bracelet, or a ring...

"*We're all down here, George, you've got to RUN . . .*" the shadow inside said.

And George ran.

"I made us ice-cream floats," Lacey said. "It's *vegan* ice cream and – well, vegan everything, but they're surprisingly good and . . ." She paused, holding a long dessert spoon in midair, and frowned at George. "What's up?"

"Nothing!" George said, too loud. In honesty he couldn't decide if he was trembling with fear or with triumph. What he'd seen in the changing rooms . . . But he'd *not* screamed, had he? He'd faced up to the terror, sort of. So now he grinned, took a big, cream-moustache-making gulp of his float, put the glass back down and—

"George!" Lacey exclaimed, as the ornate glass tipped over. At once creamy soda pooled across the kitchen counter, spilled over the edge and began to drip rapidly onto the floor.

"Oh," George said. But he *wasn't* independent enough,

and as she hurried across the kitchen he didn't move, just stood there awkwardly. When she returned with reams of paper towel in her hand, he just looked blankly at her.

"Er – *you* best wipe it up then!" she scolded. "I'm not Mum."

"Right," George said, and bent down to wipe at the spreading puddle. He was clumsy, the paper towels disintegrating into pieces before he'd gotten far at all.

Standing above him, Lacey tutted.

"I used to have to clean the table after every meal," she said. "You don't have to do it at all."

"I'm trying," George said, annoyed, knowing that if Mum or Dad had been there he probably would've kept looking helpless until one of them cleaned up for him.

With this uncomfortable thought in the back of his mind, he snatched another kitchen towel from her, got down on his hands and knees and . . .

"What's this?" he asked, and picked up a soggy leaflet. The text was smudged, and water spots were blooming across the paper. Lacey and George laid it out on the table, and quickly grew quiet.

"It's a *Missing Child* poster," she said softly. "Uncle Zeedie said he'd not heard of the case. Unless he's . . ." she trailed off, and gazed at the locked door in the hallway.

"What?"

"Well . . . unless he's lying. Like you said he was."

George stared at the *Missing Child* poster. Uncle Zeedie lying about missing children? It led to some horrible thoughts. But then he saw something worse. Something he couldn't help but recognise. His hands, already trembling, began to shake.

"What's wrong?" Lacey said.

George controlled his hands, looked her in the eye.

"I think you have to come and see this."

—Chapter Thirteen—

"Which one do you mean?" Lacey said impatiently, as George hovered by the lockers. He was practically skipping from one foot to the other.

"It's this one, this first one, it . . . it was open before."

George fell silent. All the lockers were shut, and didn't look like they'd been opened in a long time. The first locker, the one George was standing by, looked even more rusted over than the others. Again Lacey felt that mixture of frustration and anxiety for her strange kid brother. Exasperated, she stepped forwards and pulled at the door.

It was jammed, rusted shut.

"This has been closed for time," she said with a glare, daring him to say it was a practical joke. But he didn't, and so she hefted at the door as hard as she could. When, finally, it jerked open, the small hooped handle bent her finger sideways so hard that she swore. Inside there was . . .

"Nothing. There's nothing here," Lacey said critically. And George – who'd actually had a hand in front of his eyes – looked.

"No, wait . . ." he said, and looked closer. "Wait – there is. There is, look."

Lacey took out her phone and put on the torch. He was putting her on edge right now, wasting her time when she could be out meeting up with Rose, when she could . . .

"What's this?" she murmured, and leaned in closer. There, at the very bottom of the locker's metal pit, something barely glimmered with a plastic shine. How George had been able to see it without sticking his head right in she didn't know. Lacey doubted that he could open the door in the first place. She reached in and picked it out.

It was a ring, the kind of plastic jewellery you'd get with a Barbie magazine. Lacey held it up, and then her eyes travelled past it to her brother. George, whose hands were shaking only very slightly now, was holding up the *Missing Child* poster.

MISSING CHILD:
HAVE YOU SEEN BETHANY?

Below this grim title was the photo of a girl, a school photo. She was smiling adorably at the camera, and – in a way that she must've thought was *proper* slick – was holding her fingers out to show off the plastic ring she'd clearly smuggled in.

It was this plastic ring.

"Okay," said Lacey. "Now you're freaking me out."

"I think there might be something else," said George.

"Here," said George. "I don't even know how you'd look in the drains, though."

They were in his bathroom. The floor was warm beneath his socks, and the marble glimmered reassuringly around them. The horrors of the night before seemed distant, and even after the strangeness of the changing rooms, he felt lingering doubts. But Lacey, as harsh as she could be, didn't suffer from doubts.

"Out the way," she ordered. "I had to help Dad unblock the sink last time, remember?"

She knelt down by the sink and fiddled beneath the basin. After a moment, there was a stale smell, water spilled out onto the floor, and Lacey handed him a u-shaped plastic pipe.

"Is this what you saw?"

In the pipe, its face mouldered and chipped away as though tortured, was the head of a plastic Barbie doll. They both stared at it.

And then a voice they really didn't want to hear right then called to them from downstairs.

"George? Larissa? Are you there?"

It was Uncle Zeedie.

—Chapter Fourteen—

Lacey didn't hesitate. She shoved the pipe into George's hands, hissing, "Fix that back!" before hurrying out to the landing.

"Larissa . . ." Uncle Zeedie was standing halfway up the stairs, his face unreadable. "Where are you going?"

"Nowhere," Lacey said, then corrected herself. "Actually, me and George were going to take a walk through the woods."

"The woods," Uncle Zeedie repeated, and frowned. He was thinner, paler than ever. "You should be careful. It's easy to get lost in the woods here."

Lacey forced a smile, forced it to be as reassuring as possible. "We'll be fine."

"I was wondering . . . do you plan on seeing your friends today?"

"Yes, actually," she admitted. "We'll probably hang out at one of their houses."

"I wonder where they live?"

Well that's a strange question, Lacey thought. Was it just her or was there a sinister edge to his voice? *Don't be ridiculous,* she thought. But what about the ring that child wore? What about the doll stuffed into a drain?

"They're not far," she said lightly. "I mean, I'll be going soon, so—"

"Ah," Uncle Zeedie said, "not a problem. I was wondering if perhaps you would like to play a board game with myself and George this evening. However, if it's just the two of us, then—"

"No!" Lacey shouted it before she could stop herself. Uncle Zeedie blinked in surprise, but she didn't care; she was not going to leave her kid brother alone with him.

"What I meant was," she said more calmly, "me and George are going to see my friends now. We'll be back before tonight. Maybe we could play something then?"

"Oh," Uncle Zeedie said. "Well . . . good."

Lacey stared at him, and for a moment she wanted to show him the poster, the ring, the Barbie head; wanted to ask him why he was lying to them. But then George appeared from his room. He looked stressed, with water all down his trousers.

"What?" he said grumpily when he saw them stare.

"Why can't you aim properly, George?" Lacey snapped. "Go and change your trousers, before we go up the hill."

"So . . . why . . . are . . . we . . . doing . . . this?"

The going was slow. George, the sweet-eating screen fiend, took *for ever*. With his habit lately of screaming at unseen ghosts, Lacey didn't dare leave him for too long, and so the walk soon consisted of a *lot* of her waiting as he stumbled up the path, sweating *way* more than a twelve-year-old should sweat, and muttering curses to himself. *Probably in Orcish*, she thought with a grimace.

"I've told you already," Lacey said, pausing to watch her brother struggle over a fallen branch, "Uncle Zeedie said there's signal up there. We'll ring Mum, or Dad."

At that, George brightened and sped up, albeit still grunting and cursing. In fact, Lacey noticed, he seemed to be the noisiest thing around. No birds sang in the trees. No leaves rustled under tiny paws. When they at last reached the *Ega ivin* clearing where the tree stumps were, Lacey looked around at the ancient Welsh woods, as tangled as rainforest, and couldn't spot a single sign of animal or insect life.

"What is this place?" George said, looking doubtfully at the circles of rocks.

"It's where Rose and that lot hang out."

"It's a bit—"

"Creepy? What a massive surprise."

Frustratingly though, George had a point. Not only were there no trees in this small area, even the canopy seemed to avoid it, as though the surrounding trees had strained to grow their branches away. It made this the brightest spot in the woods. Lacey couldn't help but wonder just *who* had made it like this.

"It is strange," she murmured. "These stool-shaped rocks they were sitting on – I hadn't realised how old they were.

And that sign, *Egaivin*. What is that, old Gaelic or something?"

"And the bigger rocks," George added, "who put them there? It's like mini Stonehenge."

Lacey saw what he meant. Each tall boulder was lined up perfectly behind the smaller stools. They were formed of a blueish stone, a lot of which was covered in vines, and they all stood leaning towards the middle, like slender giants bowing to an altar.

Lacey looked at George curiously. A question had just occurred to her.

"Are you ... seeing something here, George?" she asked.

George glanced up, his face reddening quickly.

"No," he said defensively. "It's just creepy."

"Not like at the train station. Or last night, in the house."

Now he scowled. "Don't make fun," he muttered.

"I'm not making fun, George," she pressed. "Honestly, I'm not. I just ... I just don't get what ..."

"Do you remember my Special Guesses?" he snapped finally.

"Yeah," Lacey said with a chuckle. "How could I forget? I dared say anything to Mum and Dad and they'd tell me to mind my own business. Then you'd say where you thought next door went on holiday and it was all *'Ooh, George's Special Guesses!'*"

"I knew you'd be like this—" George began to bite. But then he paused, and allowed her half a smile. "Yeah, it probably was like that for you. But the thing was ... a lot of them were right, Lacey, you had to admit that. It was like . . . when I won that poetry competition in Year 6, Miss Thompson said I could peel back the mask of life."

"Eesh, she always was a fruit loop," Lacey said, rolling her eyes. George giggled.

"Okay, she was a bit, but what she meant was I was sensitive—"

"Dad called it 'weepy'—"

"Yeah," George said, but his chuckle this time was pained, and instantly Lacey regretted the jibe. "Yeah, but . . . since Mum and Dad started *hating* each other like this . . . it's like it's all been peeled back *too* much."

Lacey looked away for a moment.

"George," she said softly, "Mum and Dad . . . they *always* hated each other. You just couldn't see it before."

George stopped and stared at her, his bottom lip quivering. *Buck up*, Lacey thought savagely for one moment, *it's nothing like I had to deal with.* But then she caught herself. She was being unfair.

"All I'm saying," she said gently, "is that . . . is there any chance – you know when you started screaming at the train station last week? And you know last night, in your bedroom? Is there any chance you were just . . . reliving the horror of finding that hatred out?"

To his credit, George thought about this for a long moment. He scratched his glasses, then cleaned them, and for a moment looked much older than twelve. Then he nodded.

"It's not just that. But it definitely made a difference," he accepted. "It was horrible. Every time I get the . . .

the Feeling, the thing at the middle of it is seeing Mum and Dad scream like that at each other."

Now Lacey wanted to cry. Part of her had tried to shield George from that fury, even when she resented him not being aware of it. Out of nowhere, she gave him a hug. His arms flailed about for a moment . . . then they rested by his side. *George is rubbish at hugs*, she thought with a grin.

And then, just as she was about to suggest they continue on up the hill, George added, "I searched about that clock at the train station, you know. It used to be where they kept the gallows, where they executed people. The bodies used to hang right in front of where the old clock is now, right where I saw them. Hung, drawn and quartered, it said."

And with that, George carried on up the hill, leaving Lacey speechless.

— Chapter Fifteen —

They didn't stop again until the top of the hill. Well, *Lacey* didn't stop. She kept yomping on, even when George had to rest, taking big strides into the distance like some merry bloody Tom Bombadil while he was slumped over a tree branch gasping out "STOP . . . STOP . . ." in ever-weakening tones. Eventually, staggering up the last of the muddy path, George took the final step onto lovely, familiar tarmac, and crouched down, gulping breaths like each one might be his last.

Then he looked up.

"Is this it?" he moaned. "Seriously? It's a bunch of shacks!" But Lacey had already walked ahead, checking her phone for signal, and didn't respond. "What about Dad!" George called after her, hurrying to catch up yet again. "Are you going to call Dad?"

The village – if it could even be called that – was silent and eerily run-down. The buildings were either abandoned or incomplete, with boarded-up windows or sometimes not even that, just holes in the walls that revealed a dilapidated brick shell behind it. Eventually they reached a clothes shop, only to find it *very* closed, one tired-looking mannequin behind a dust-thickened window, dressed in an outfit that looked faded and old.

The next shop was an estate agents. *BARKER'S HOUSING* the sign read, then underneath it, in ornate, handwritten letters, *Elegant Living*. In the window were adverts for houses that presumably weren't built yet, because instead of photographs there were a series of artist's renditions of swanky-looking houses set amongst fairy-like trees. A thick coat of grime clung to these pictures, but something was still familiar about them.

"Hey Lacey," George said. "What do you think of these..."

He was interrupted by the tinkle of a shop door bell. Lacey had gone in through the last door on the right, leaving him completely alone on this silent, creepy street. With a sudden jolt of fear, George hurried on, to see the sign which said:

ROSE'S STORES

"You are *joking*!" George roared. It was the shop they'd pulled up outside when they first arrived here; the shack Dad had nipped inside to buy their chocolate. And he knew why Lacey had gone straight for it.

"Lacey! You just dragged me all the way up here so you could meet that Rose! Are you even gonna ring Dad..."

George burst through the shop door, sending the rusted bell above rattling furiously. At once, his voice died away. There was nothing but the sound of a radio in another room – no sign of anyone.

"Lacey?" he said again.

The shop was well stocked, even if it didn't seem to have any customers. Brand new crates of drinks and crisps lined the shelves. He moved from aisle to aisle, and found her standing by the magazines.

"Look," she said, quietly.

Unlike the snacks, the magazines hadn't been restocked at all. Instead, their glossy pages were curled up with age, the pictures and font on their front covers strangely out of date. The magazine Lacey was staring at was clearly for horror fans, its cover art showing a cartoon drawing of a hand holding a bloodied knife. George *hated* horror, and was about to do what he always did, which was pretend to scoff about how cheesy it was... when he read the headlines.

Neither of them said a word.

—THE BLOOD TEXTS—
MONTHLY MURDER AND MAYHEM

THIS ISSUE:
WITCH CROSSWORDS!
THE VAMPIRE'S SAVAGE COUSIN!
BREW YOUR OWN BLOOD!
AND . . .

SERIAL KILLER IN THE FAMILY:
TRUE STORIES OF THE WORST KIND

> *Cassie knew her elder brother wasn't always normal. But nothing prepared her for what was in the basement freezer . . .*
>
> **SEE PAGE 12**
>
> *Toby couldn't lie to himself any more. His mother's new boyfriends always went missing, right before she baked a whole batch of . . .*
>
> **SEE PAGE 14**
>
> *Farook was scared of her dad. She didn't know just how scared she should be, until she found the jars filled with . . .*
>
> **SEE PAGE 22**
>
> **ALSO INSIDE – A FULL HOW-TO-FIND GUIDE, THE ONLY WAY YOU'LL BE SURE:**
> **DO YOU KNOW A SERIAL KILLER?**

"You know Rose and her friends . . ." Lacey murmured. "The way they talked about Uncle Zeedie, it was like they thought he was one. A serial killer, I mean."

She turned to look at George. He stared back, doubt in his pale, pinched face.

"It can't b—" he began, when a clattering noise from the other end of the shop made them jump.

"Hello? Lacey said. She went to the end of the aisle,

just in time to see the shop door slam close, footsteps outside walking quickly away.

"Hello?" she called again, hurrying to the door.

"Wait—" George began, but she was already opening it.

"Who's there?" she called. The street seemed abandoned, silent again. Then, from around the side of the shop came the sound of a door being opened. Lacey ran now, past the shop, past the Community Noticeboard. In the car park behind it, a man was urgently trying to unlock a green van...

"Hey!" Lacey shouted. The man looked nervously over his shoulder, made to get inside, and she shouted again. "Who are you?"

At last, the man's shoulders slumped. He climbed back down, and faced her.

"I'm sorry," he apologised. "I didn't mean to startle you. My name's Bill. I'm just a delivery driver. When Rose isn't covering the shop, she asks me to drop the supplies round the back."

"I saw your van before," Lacey said. "When we were driving to Uncle Zeedie's."

At the mention of Uncle Zeedie, the man seemed to shudder. "You mean the big house at the bottom. Yep, I deliver there. The man likes everything left by the gate so as he's not... disturbed."

Lacey eyed the man suspiciously. He looked old, and tired. He was wearing a delivery uniform, green jumper and jeans, and they all hung baggy on him, as though his body had been squeezed thin. His white hair and beard were untidy and overgrown. As he climbed down from the van, he stooped, having to rest one hand on the vehicle for support.

"Why did you run away, then?" she demanded. *Especially when you blatantly can't run.*

"I . . ." Bill's eyes glanced to the Community Noticeboard. Lacey hadn't looked properly at it before, but hanging from it were six *Missing Child* posters. "I figured you were staying at the big house at the bottom of the valley. With . . . *him*."

"Uncle Zeedie," Lacey said.

Bill nodded. "He's very strict about privacy. I'm the only person from outside with access to that house. If you tell him I was talking to you and I lose my job . . ." He trailed off for a moment, as if unsure what to say. "If I lose my job there won't be anyone left who can uncover the truth. The truth about the missing children."

Lacey heard a gasp behind her, and looked around. It was George.

"It can't . . ." Lacey said doubtfully. "It just seems impossible. My mum and dad have known Uncle Zeedie for years. And yes, he's acting strange, but . . . I mean, what's the evidence it's anything more messed up than that?"

For a moment the man looked torn, as though he didn't want to say anything else. Then finally his eyes slid ashamedly away from hers to the ground.

"I live in the next village along," he said quietly. "It's not a rich village, none of the villages around here are. When they started to build this place, we were all excited.

Thought it might bring some money to the area. And for a while," he gestured to his uniform, "it did."

"Then children started to go missing. It seemed like too few to mean anything at first, you know. And like I say, the villages have been going through bad times. Kids don't want to live here. People just assumed they'd run away. But *four*? Four in such a short space of time . . . and it only began when *he* moved in."

"We've found some things," Lacey said as this sunk in. "Some things that might belong to the missing children. They were in Uncl– in his house."

"That doesn't surprise me." The man shook his head. "The more we looked into the missing children, the darker the truth began to seem. They'd all been playing near that place, or been on trips to the Sink just before they disappeared. They'd all talked about seeing big houses, about a strange man who lived in the biggest house, right on the valley floor. I spoke to Rose and her friends, and they said they'd seen him out late at night, this man. It had been raining when they were messing around in the woods. They found some shelter near his house, and one of them said they heard a horrible noise, more like a pig than a human. And the boy, the grumpy one called River? He saw Zeedie carrying a small body into the house."

And there it was. The words that made this into something more real, more dreadful than it had ever been before. An actual accusation, something that couldn't be misconstrued, couldn't be imagined. With a sick feeling in her stomach,

Lacey turned to George, then back to Bill.

"I'm sorry," the old man said sincerely. "It's not a nice thing to hear about your uncle."

"He's not my uncle," Lacey said coldly. "That's just what we call him."

"Family's family," said Bill. "There's no feeling like it. If they get cut, and you hurt? That's family."

He was right. Lacey felt sick. It was a horrible, horrible feeling, hearing something so heinous about someone she'd always called 'uncle'.

"Has anyone got any *proof*?" she asked, and hated how desperate she sounded.

"That's what we need – a body," said Bill. "They must be in there. Zeedie never leaves his estate. Whatever's happened, it happened at that house. Is there anywhere you haven't explored yourselves?"

"There's a basement," George said, "but he said he lost the key."

"Find it," Bill said. His breath was growing short, his face pale. "You have . . . to find it. Now, I don't want him to see me with you, else we'll all be in danger. I'd better go."

They watched as he opened up the door again. He was about to get in when George blurted out, "Can't somebody call the police or something?"

Bill stopped, his eyes haunted.

"Do you think they didn't? Like I said, these villages are poor. Nobody's interested in our problems. Especially not compared with the kind of man who can build houses like that." He sighed. "Find that key. Open that basement. I hope you can find the answers about that monster you call your uncle."

— Chapter Sixteen —

"*. . . on the third budget . . . and it's just not . . . work, unless . . . meetings all day . . .*"

"Dad?"

"*Hold . . . a minute* – Lacey?"

"Dad!"

"*Lacey, I . . . every . . . a . . . ight?*"

"Dad!"

"Lacey? George? Can you hear me?"

"We can hear you, Dad!"

"Good! So you have got signal there!"

"Not really, we had to—"

"How's it going, you . . . an amazing time? *Sorry . . . a minute John, I'll—*"

"No, Dad, you've got to come!"

"*Two secs, John, I'll be back with you* . . . Kids, I'm so sorry, I'm snowed under right now, can I call you back? Bes . . . es, you don't nee . . . be updating me . . . ou . . . njoy . . ."

"Dad! Dad! It's about Uncle Zeedie! Dad!"

Static.

"... No, Mum you've got to listen! It's about Uncle Zeedie."

"What is it?"

"Well... He's just being... weird."

"Lacey, I don't... you saying tha... know I...on't."

"Argh, Mum! But, Mum, he's—"

"... known...our Uncle Zee... ng time... ent through a very difficult childhood and... b... g... because of this."

"Yeah, Mum, you're not listening. I met some kids round here and—"

"You're... upposed to... think for yourself... idn't your dad say that?"

"We couldn't get through to him!"

"... a surprise. One weekend is... I'm asking... nd he won't... sick and tired of..."

"Mum! Mum!"

Static.

By the time they'd given up calling their parents, Lacey's phone battery was low and the sun was beginning to set. Rather than cut through the woods, they followed the main road that wound its way down the crater-like valley, growing more hungry and tired with every step. It took them *hours*, and of course, George moaned the *whole* way – first about the walk, and then about Lacey's plan.

"I don't like it," he whinged for the umpteenth time, setting Lacey's teeth on edge. "So I've got to play a game with him while you disappear? What if he asks me where you are?"

"I'm not disappearing," Lacey replied (for the umpteenth time), "I'll just say I want some time alone."

"Why can't *you* stay with Uncle Zeedie and *I* look?"

"Really," she said dryly. "You'll go down into that dark and spooky basement where all the bodies of kids are buried."

"I could do that," he said sulkily.

"George, we've just walked up a hill and you look like you've been fighting in the trenches! No, you play the game with Zeedie. I'll find the key and search the basement. We've got to do this."

George looked sulkily back at her, but didn't argue.

"What if you find something?" he said.

"Then we get out of there and we get help as quickly as we..."

Lacey trailed off as the house grew closer. Standing in the doorway was a tall, thin, sinister figure.

"It's late," Uncle Zeedie said coldly. "I was beginning to think you might be hurt."

–Chapter Seventeen–

> **DO YOU KNOW A SERIAL KILLER?**
>
> *If you answer mostly a)s You might be the paranoid killer yourself, but your suspect is not.*
> *If you answer mostly b)s Your suspect may be responsible for a maiming here or there, but all-out murder would be a stretch, let alone a series of them.*
> *If you answer mostly c)s Then GET OUT GET OUT GET OUT, you are in contact with a murderous fiend!*

A power shower and a warm meal was the worst thing they could've had.

The food was actually pretty good – a veggie soup with a nice chilli heat, and some posh bread. Her hair drying under a warm towel, the cold oozing from her bones, Lacey began to feel cosy enough to have severe doubts about her plan. The survey in *The Blood Texts* didn't help. After the shock of the front page, the questionnaire itself turned out to be one of those stupid multiple-choice quizzes, the sort that said *'If you picked mostly a)s then that dreamboat is yours!'* and *'Mostly c)s? U R destined for glamour #popqueen!'* Even after everything, it's silliness made Lacey's fears seem childish.

. . . And then she read some of the questions.

> **1. Are they**
> **a)** Focused and driven, **b)** Scatty but lovable, or **c)** Distracted and staring into the distance?
> **2. Do they often have strange scratches or bruises that they have trouble explaining?**
> **a)** No, **b)** Yes, but only because they have a chaotic life anyway, or **c)** Yes – what is going on with them?
> **3. Are they a)** Cool as a cucumber, **b)** Unemotional beings but ultimately filled with love, or **c)** Cold, awkward, and prone to sudden fits of anger?

"Uncle Zeedie doesn't have sudden fits of anger," George objected, leaning over the magazine. He was even less motivated than Lacey, stuffing himself like he'd just returned from war. Only once had he looked up, suddenly, at the basement door. Then he'd ignored Lacey's quizzical stare, had plunged his gob back into food, unwilling to say what had caught his attention.

"You didn't see him the night after I came back late," Lacey whispered back. "He looked like he wanted to throttle me."

"You make Mum look like that all the time! *And* she's always forgetting why she came into a room and stuff. Is *she* a serial killer?"

"Just think about the whole questionnaire though," Lacey insisted. "Here – 'Do they go out secretly at night?' He snuck out last night!"

"So did you!"

"Oh, f—"

At that moment Uncle Zeedie walked by the door, and Lacey stuffed the magazine back in her jacket. George got back to eating, looking readier than ever for a catnap.

"Look," she said at last, "Number five: Are they a) Unimpeachably honest, b) Forgetful of the truth, or c) Constantly caught up in a web of lies? Question seven: 'Is their house a) Clean, b) Messy but lovable, or c) Cold and barren, yet still contains hidden pieces of 'evidence' that may or may not connect with local murder cases. Ten: 'Are they letting strange things slip around the house, such as mouldy food or—' Mouldy food! Thirteen: 'a strong smell of sour milk—' I mean, come on, George! Sour milk!"

But George had had it. He was warm, and he was tired, and he'd eaten. Again he glanced at the basement door, but he didn't say anything.

Glowering at him, she finished the survey and checked the results page:

If you answer mostly c)s Then GET OUT GET OUT GET OUT, you are in contact with a . . .

"What's that?"

Lacey slammed the magazine into the inside of her jacket, but of course it was far too late. She looked up guiltily as Uncle Zeedie stood over her, that awkward smile on his face. She opened her mouth to reply, but couldn't think of what to say. "Nothing," she said in the end.

His smile froze into shards. "I would really like to see it," he said.

Still she didn't answer. For a moment she was sure, *sure*, that he was about to snatch out for it, but he didn't. Instead he held up a box.

"Yahtzee tonight?" he asked. "I used to play with your mother and father."

Lacey sighed, glancing at George. Of course, he was staring down at the table, the big coward.

"Is it okay if I join you later?" she asked. "I'm still pretty tired from the walk."

Again, that fractured smile. But Uncle Zeedie nodded stiffly, and gestured out to the room. Lacey noticed more scratches on his arms.

"That's fine," he said in his high voice. "This isn't a prison. You can do what you like."

"Thanks, Uncle Zeedie," Lacey replied as nicely as she could. "I knew you'd understand."

— Chapter Eighteen —

"Tell you what, George," said Uncle Zeedie, "why don't I make us some smoothies?"

As Lacey hurried upstairs and Uncle Zeedie went to the kitchen, George found himself alone, standing in the middle of the slightly damp living room, scratching his dry throat and staring unhappily into space. A security light outside was on the blink. It flickered on to reveal the swimming pool and night-muddied woods beyond. Then it flickered off, turning the windows into huge mirrors, reflecting the room around him.

He was annoyed. Why couldn't Lacey just relax for one night? They'd walked for *miles*, his feet hurt, and . . .

And I really don't want that door opened.

George blinked. His traitorous eyes drifted to the ominous basement door – then darted away like mice beneath a fridge. He hadn't been conscious of it until the man at the shop, Bill, told them to look for evidence down there. But now, he was afraid of that door. Things were waiting behind it, brooding. Angry, *furious* things that wanted vengeance. He shuddered involuntarily, then shuddered again at the soft footsteps that padded into the room behind him.

"Here you go," Uncle Zeedie said, grinning as he handed over the freshly made smoothie, revealing his white, square teeth.

"Thanks, Uncle Zeeds," George said politely. The smoothie looked vomitous; beige and lumpy. He took the drink, and something glanced off the inside of the glass before drifting out of sight. He pretended to sip, and looked for a place to put the drink down.

"Wait – I forgot coasters," Uncle Zeedie said, striding to where a stack of unused drinks mats sat on an otherwise empty shelf. The faulty security light flickered off, George glanced to the huge windows, saw the room reflected behind him... and froze.

He didn't move until Uncle Zeedie returned. Zeedie took the drink from him and shot him a concerned look, although George didn't quite see it as he was still staring at the reflection of the room in the glass of the big window.

"Are you alright, George? You're shivering."

"I..." George began, and didn't know what else to say.

"I tell you what – I have a spare snood. Have you heard of snoods? It has *never* been worn, I think you would love it. It's just up in my room."

That brought George to his senses. He shook his head, coughing slightly at the dryness in the back of his throat.

"Honestly," he insisted, "it's fine, it..."

It was too late. Uncle Zeedie had turned, was already walking up the stairs, towards his room. Walking up... towards Lacey.

— Chapter Nineteen —

The first thing Lacey noticed about Uncle Zeedie's bedroom was how boring, how bland it was. The second was that the blandness was creepy in itself.

There were no pictures. No photographs, nothing. In fact, there was no sign that this room had even been lived in. It was like an unused hotel room, with a perfectly made bed. Not knowing where to look, she searched first in the drawers beneath it. Again, there was nothing but bed linen inside, except...

Sticking out from beneath the linen was a piece of paper, ***MISSING CHILD*** stamped across the top. With that hollow feeling in the pit of her stomach, Lacey pulled it out and saw a boy with brown skin, holding a mermaid Barbie doll. Lacey pulled open the second drawer and... there it was. An old deadbolt key.

She'd found it.

"*Er, er, so we'll play in a minute yeah, Uncle Zeeds?*" George shouted from the hallway.

". . . Yes, George, of course," Uncle Zeedie replied,

sounding bemused. Lacey bit back a curse – he was coming up the stairs! Without a moment to lose, she ran to a door in the corner, opened it and . . .

Dammit, it was just another bathroom! Knowing that if he came in here she'd be caught, Lacey closed the door just as Uncle Zeedie walked into the bedroom. She was single-minded when necessary and, stuck in this bathroom, she used the opportunity to look for more evidence. She opened the medicine cabinet . . . and paused.

There was *another* deadbolt key in there. She opened the next cabinet door . . . and found another one. Just how many keys did Uncle Zeedie have? She dared to open the door to the bedroom slightly, and peered through. Uncle Zeedie was still there, looking through the drawers on one side of his fitted wardrobe. He looked puzzled, reached inside and removed . . .

Another key. Just what the hell was he doing with all these keys? Whatever it was, they weren't what he was looking for, because Uncle Zeedie put the key back inside, closed the drawer, slid the wardrobe door over to the other side and . . .

A strange noise came from his throat. Lacey wasn't sure what it was – a stifled giggle or what. For a moment he stayed there, not moving, just staring into the open wardrobe, although what he was staring at she couldn't see. At last, he reached up to the high shelf and took down something woolly. Then he slid shut the door, and walked back out.

"I'll be down in a minute, George!" he called downstairs.

Lacey should run for it now, she knew. But she *had* to know what was in that wardrobe. She heard footsteps climbing the stairs – not down but *up*, up to the second floor where Uncle Zeedie's office was. Now was her chance. She hurried silently across the bedroom to the wardrobe, slid open the door and...

It was all she could do not to cry out. Hanging in the wardrobe, facing out as if on display, was a white shirt *covered* in blood. Not blood from a small cut, not blood from an accident.

The kind of blood that could only come from slaughter.

—Chapter Twenty—

While Lacey was stuck in the bathroom, and Uncle Zeedie was staring at the bloodied shirt in his wardrobe, George wasn't doing well at all. The security light was still flickering on and off outside, the view through those huge windows blinking alternately between the swimming pool outside and the room behind him. He knew what he was seeing in that reflection was not reality. Yet, like always when the Feeling struck him, George could not tear his eyes away.

It was the basement door, the one George really wanted Lacey to leave alone. It was closed now, when he turned to look at it. But when that faulty security light flickered off and the windows turned into mirrors, the reflection would show that door...

...wide open.

"*George,*" a voice whispered from the darkness. "*We're all down here, George.*"

George turned, glanced sharply at the door behind him. It *was* closed. That smell drifted across his nostrils again –

God, that smell, like sour milk. Why was it everywhere here? Again the light flickered off outside, and again he couldn't help but look at the reflection in front of him, at the open door behind.

"Look, George," the voice urged. *"LOOK OUT..."*

"I'm fine," George muttered to himself, his head pounding, a bead of cold sweat tracing ice down his back. He took an unsteady step towards the window, just as the outside light flickered back on to reveal the swimming pool, the woods and...

George frowned, staring through the window at the swimming pool outside. Had he just seen something out there? Not the Feeling, although that was here, but something else actually *out there*, beyond the pool? Something that had moved?

"Look, George. LOOK OUT THERE."

Forcing back the vomit, the dizziness, the Feeling, George stumbled closer to the window until his face was almost pressed against the glass. There was nothing out there now, nothing he could see. Behind him, footsteps raced down the stairs, and his sister hissed his name.

"George? George! I've got the key! I'm going down there now. GEORGE!"

George didn't hear, not quite. He was too busy searching outside. It was real, the thing he'd seen out there, he was positive it was. Not until Lacey sighed in exasperation at her dopey little brother, not until the key was thrust into the lock and the security light flickered out, turning the window into a mirror once more, did he see her unlock the basement door and turn the handle.

"Lacey," he muttered, "Don't open that—"

But it was too late. And as his sister opened the basement door, the ghosts rushed out towards him, and George collapsed, drowning in reflections of the eager dead.

Chapter Twenty-One

The basement black was absolute, the kind of dark to lose your limbs. The air was foul: sweet curdling milk, and something worse. Lacey shut the door behind her, and switched on her phone torch to reveal a flight of dusty wooden stairs and a dirty concrete floor at their base. A dark red stain had bloomed across that concrete. It looked like an abattoir.

Bucking up, Lacey descended the steps and scanned left and right, ears pricked for any sound. This basement was small, way smaller than she would've expected given how big the house was, almost like it had been cut off. She heard Zeedie talking upstairs, his voice sounding concerned, although she couldn't make out any words, and...

Shuffle.

"Shi—" Lacey wheeled around to race back upstairs but cracked her shin on the second step. A yell of pain blurted from her throat before she could smother it, the *Blood Texts* magazine flew out of her hands, and Lacey toppled onto the stairs, hand clamped over her mouth, afraid to even move a muscle. Through the door she heard Uncle Zeedie's cold voice grow closer.

"... get you some water ..." he said, before his footsteps faded and his words mangled into noise. Again there was that shuffling sound, but now, less panicked, Lacey didn't move. She just listened.

Shuffle.

That's not a person.

Creeping back down the stairs, Lacey walked across the basement, torchlight reaching out ahead of her. As evil as the air was down here, there *was* a draught, the faintest breeze coming from somewhere unseen. The shuffling sound was that of paper being ruffled, which meant there had to be a desk or some files or ...

"Got it," Lacey whispered aloud. It was a noticeboard, hanging above a set of metal shelves on the wall ahead. On the board were posters, *loads* of them, their corners curled and fluttering gently in the breeze, although where that breeze came from she couldn't work out, and why anyone would want to hang posters down here she didn't ...

One step closer and Lacey's breath stopped. They were *Missing Child* posters, all of them, and blood was spattered across every one. Pinned between the posters were newspaper cuttings: 'Boy, 16, Still Missing', 'Hunt Widens For Teenage Girl', 'Family Still Searching For Their 9-Year-Old Son'. All together they formed an evil wallpaper, and as if this weren't grim enough, somebody had written all over the lot, deranged graffiti in letters fat and wild, the ink splotched and seeping, as though the pen had split from the writer's frenzied scribbling.

Gutted her in the rain
Squealed like a pig hahahahahahahaha
Ate their hearts for I am the Angel of Death

Horrified, Lacey took a step back, the beam of light glinting down the metal shelves as she did. And *god*, the shelves were worse. *There* were the clothes, bloodstained rags. *There* were the weapons, evil-looking hooks, long knives, screwdrivers and even a fire poke, all of them rusted.

And *there* was the meat, buckets of it; bloody and mouldering flesh.

Gagging, she staggered back, a low, strangled sound in her throat. They had to run. They had to get away, as quickly as they could. Even just yesterday it had seemed impossible – but now she knew.

Uncle Zeedie was a serial killer.

Chapter Twenty-Two

"George? George."

George opened his eyes. Somewhere in the back of his mind a voice screamed "*RUN*" one last time. Then it was lost.

"You had me worried there, George," somebody chuckled. "I came down and you'd collapsed to the floor."

George rubbed his head, still groggy. He'd been moved back to the chair, which was a relief because the room was listing left and right, and the smell of sour milk still choked at his nostrils. But the ghosts, the visions; whatever they were, they'd gone. Only Uncle Zeedie stood over him, smiling his jagged smile. In his hand was a new glass of his hideous smoothie mixture.

"Go on," he encouraged softly, "it's full of antioxidants. Drink up."

George stared at it, sick and scared.

"Can't... can't I just have water?"

Uncle Zeedie's smile flickered.

"I'm afraid my water filter isn't working," he said sharply.

"The water may leave a bitter taste." But he turned away all the same.

Left alone, George squeezed his head between his hands. The Feeling had gone, and his headache was just a memory, along with that awful terror of the ghosts rushing out from the basement. So many ghosts, a whole room full around him, and they had all screamed the same thing, again and again. It had been heartstopping at the time, but looking back it was a message. He shut his eyes, trying to make sense of just what that message meant. Somewhere, very softly, a door clicked shut, and footsteps hurried quickly and quietly towards him.

"We have to get out of here *now*." It was Lacey, her whispers high and petrified. "Down there is *messed up*. We've got to go, George!"

But before George could reply, that cold, high voice spoke from the doorway.

"Larissa. I was beginning to think you had left."

Uncle Zeedie was standing in the doorway, a glass of water in his hand. George felt Lacey tense beside him. *Don't*, he silently pleaded, *don't argue, not now.*

"Yeah?" Lacey said, hostile. "And what if I do leave?"

"I beg your pardon?"

"What if I'm bored of this place now, and I want to go home tomorrow? What would you do?"

"Lacey..." George began.

Uncle Zeedie's face had gone sheet-white.

"Well, I would be disappointed, of course. I would call

your father, or perhaps arrange for a car to collect you."

"Right away?"

"Right away."

For a moment, Lacey stared at Uncle Zeedie, an open challenge in her eyes. After a moment, he corrected himself.

"Well of course it is impossible to do so immediately, as the signal is not good. I would wait until morning then make my way to the top of the hill and call from there."

Lacey raised her eyebrows, smiling angrily.

"Right," she said. "So you'd get me and George to wait till tomorrow, but *then* you'd take us to—"

"Lacey—" George pleaded.

"Only you," Uncle Zeedie said quietly.

"What?"

"Only yourself, Lacey. If George wanted to stay here, I would not let your dissatisfaction end his holiday."

"George would be coming too."

"Lacey," George urged again, and Lacey glared at him, a mixture of fear and betrayal on her face.

"George?" she said through gritted teeth. And George didn't know what to say. After a moment's silence, Uncle Zeedie spoke again.

"It would be impolite of me to force George into some kind of Sophie's Choice, Larissa. I would merely say that—"

"Oh ffff's sake, why are you always so polite?! What is *wrong* with you?"

Uncle Zeedie stared, his eyes now frozen shards. At last he said, "I can see you are feeling hostility towards me.

Why don't I get some snacks, and you both discuss it while I'm gone?"

He turned away, closing the kitchen doors behind him. Immediately Lacey turned on George.

"George!" she hissed. "We need to get out of here!"

"No," George said. He swallowed, and couldn't meet her eye. "I don't want to leave, Lacey. I don't want to go out there."

Chapter Twenty-Three

Lacey stared at her brother, utterly baffled. She had to fight the urge to grab him by the sleeve and drag him to the door.

"What the *hell* is wrong with you?!" she whispered through clenched teeth. "Didn't you hear me? Down in that basement, there's..."

She trailed off.

"There's what? You never said."

"Uncle Zeedie is a *murderer*. And if we don't get out of here now, he will kill us too."

George stared back. When he finally spoke his voice sounded older somehow, like that strange, grown-up voice he'd had in the woods.

"It doesn't make sense," he said faintly. "What I saw... it can't be him."

"*It fffffrickin is, George!*" Lacey urged. "He says he doesn't use the basement – *there's about four keys to the basement door in his bedroom.*"

"Four? Why would he have four?"

"I opened his wardrobe, George, *you stupid—*" Lacey felt

her voice shake, and breathed it steady. "His *shirt* – it was covered in blood. We. Have. To. Go."

But George shook his head, looking ill. His eyes, unable to meet Lacey's, wandered to the window.

"Those woods aren't safe."

"Who said?"

He hesitated, remembering the basement doors opening, so many dead children flooding out, all screaming and ranting and raving the same thing. "The ghosts—"

"Ghosts!" Lacey stood up and slammed a hand on the table, making George flinch back.

"There is *meat* down there, you stupid boy," she hissed, "and hooks, and posters and these *horrible* things he's written and *meat*, god, like a butcher, like . . . He killed those kids. So *shut up* with your ghosts. Right now it's windy and dark out there, and so your 'ghosts' say that *out there* is bad and *in here* is good. But they *aren't* ghosts, George. That is just you being a coward. And when it is dark *in here* later, and there's shadows, and the floors are creaking and the air feels dead? Then your 'ghosts' will wish you had the cold wind, and the noise and the birds. You will *wish* you'd listened to me."

"There aren't birds in those woods, Lacey," George said softly. "There's nothing, no animals at all."

"And then you will call for me," Lacey continued, ignoring him. "You'll cry, like you always do, and I won't be there to help you 'cos I'm *sick* of it. Who helps me? *Who helps me?!*"

"Please don't . . ." George said, and the fear in his voice

made Lacey stop. She took a breath, and looked down at her hands. They were gripping George's top, clenched knuckle-white tight. George looked heartbreakingly scared, as scared of Lacey as she was of Uncle Zeedie. She let go, and took a step back.

"Think about it, George," she pleaded with him. "Just think about the ring, and the doll, and the pamphlets, and the magazine—"

"The magazine is just making fun of weirdos."

"Yeah, well *some* weirdos are messed up!" Lacey snapped.

"*I'm* a weirdo," George said.

Lacey didn't have an answer to that.

"Please," she said, and hated the tears prickling at her eyes. "Please, George."

"Have you made your decision?"

It was Uncle Zeedie, standing in the door to the living room, that smirk on his face. Lacey didn't know how much he'd heard, and wouldn't have cared were it not for the possible repercussions on George. She knew now that she had to stop Uncle Zeedie, and to stop him she had to get help.

"George." She leaned close and whispered. "The minute you suspect something. The minute you see through *him*. Then you run away. Understand? You run away, and you don't stop. I'll be back as soon as I can. I promise I will."

"Please don't go," George said, his voice quiet, and high, and oh-so small. "It's not safe out there, Lacey."

Without another word, Lacey turned and walked out,

straight for the front door. Outside, she cut across behind the swimming pool, taking the quickest path into the woods. The air was too cold to be out without her jacket, and her phone battery was too low to rely on. Still she kept on walking, until the cold bit and the darkness swallowed, and all that was left to see was in her memory; that look of fear on her little brother's face.

Chapter Twenty-Four

"You're sure you won't play Yahtzee?" Uncle Zeedie asked.

"I'm pretty tired," George said awkwardly. He was torn between feeling bad and feeling scared. Uncle Zeedie's face was still frozen in that slight smirk. It had been like that since Lacey left. For the umpteenth time, George wondered if he'd made a terrible mistake not leaving with her.

"You're not having another dizzy spell, I hope?"

George shook his head, and they both fell into silence.

"How do you know my mum and dad?" George blurted out at last.

Uncle Zeedie stared. For one dreadful moment George pictured him saying that they were accomplices, that they assisted him in his gruesome crimes. Then he spoke, very awkwardly.

"When I was younger . . . I didn't have friends. For a long time. And then, one day, I met your dad, and he was my friend. He didn't have to be. He just was. Your mother I met later, at university. I met her before your father did. I had gone to a very prestigious university, my software company had begun to succeed, and again I found that I had no friends. Your dad came to see me, and then met your mother . . . and he visited a lot more after that."

Uncle Zeedie smiled, and despite his fears, George smiled back. He knew what that smile meant. *The Normies*, they were both thinking. Normal people with their normal lives – not like either of them. They could be good people, the Normies. But they didn't understand, wouldn't ever understand. For a moment George felt a wave of sympathy for Uncle Zeedie. Then, he heard Lacey's voice. *How can you feel sympathy for a serial killer?*

"It got easier, though?" he asked uneasily. "You made more friends as you got older?"

"No," said Zeedie, with an honesty George could've done without. "It gets harder. At least while you're young, you're forced together with people. As you get older, you have to try to meet them. And I . . . never became good at that."

"Who are your friends now?" George asked.

"There was my very best friend, the man I went into business with," Zeedie replied. "But he hasn't been the same since . . ."

He looked at George, as though debating whether to tell him something or not. Then he sighed.

"My best friend's daughter died, and since then he has shut himself away."

"That's horrible," George said. He couldn't help but think *'Did you kill her?'*, even as he felt awful for it.

Uncle Zeedie nodded, though the emotion barely showed

on his face. "Then, there's your parents. I'll for ever be grateful to them for the time they took to help me. But they are always busy, and I don't like to fuss. Especially when . . . they both would like me to take sides in their own current arguments."

That was so on the mark that George almost winced. Why did he have to understand Uncle Zeedie so well? What did that say about him?

"Besides," Uncle Zeedie said, "my business has kept me so busy that I haven't had much time for friends. Although lately . . ." He paused, again as though he was considering telling George something. But this time he didn't. "Yes," he said instead. "It was hard to achieve my success."

George stared at him. There it was again. Uncle Zeedie had just lied. He wasn't sure about what, and couldn't say how he knew, but he knew.

An idea suddenly occurred to him then, one of George's Special Guesses. It seemed unlikely, but if he was right, then it might explain why this place was so run down. It might even explain why Uncle Zeedie was lying to them. It . . . it wouldn't explain the basement, not yet. But it might be a step towards figuring that out as well. George would just need the right evidence. Could he find it himself?

"I think . . ." he said slowly, "I think I need to go to sleep."

George didn't go to sleep. He lay in bed for what seemed like hours. Finally, he heard Uncle Zeedie's footsteps walking quietly downstairs, followed by the sound of the front door opening, and being softly closed. He snuck out of his room, bare feet crushing silently into the thick landing carpet, and glimpsed over the balcony.

He was alone in the house. Uncle Zeedie's room was open, with no one inside. The faulty security light still flickered on and off through the living room windows, and George got a brief fright when he saw Uncle Zeedie's thin silhouette trudge past outside. Directly below was the basement door, and though he couldn't see it, George could feel the things behind it glowering at him, impatient.

This was a mistake, he thought, as his headache returned. *I should go to bed, hide under the covers.*

Then he turned around and climbed the stairs up to the second floor.

The sliding door to Uncle Zeedie's office squeaked as he opened it, to reveal nothing but a desk with a chair either side, a lamp on top. Already jumpy, George hurried to the desk, and pulled at the top drawer. Inside it was all business post – letters about shares, red-topped bills and official-looking bank statements. They didn't tell George much . . . except that Uncle Zeedie's business had been doing badly. Judging from the threatening tone of the letters, *really* badly.

George shut the top drawer and pulled at the next. This was completely useless, nothing but stationery and memory sticks. Frustrated, he was closing it when the front door opened downstairs.

He froze, breath held in fear. The sliding door was slightly ajar, showing the second-floor hallway, the loft entrance in the ceiling, and spiral stairs plunging to darkness ahead. Picturing Uncle Zeedie striding out from that dark, face grim and hands outstretched, George opened the next drawer. It was crammed to the brim with postcards and Christmas cards. Taking out the top one, he saw it was from someone calling themself "*WB*". Inside was a photograph of an older girl, around Lacey's age, laughing as she decorated a Christmas tree. George caught one sentence:

> "... *Izzy has been great, I couldn't have gotten through the funeral without her* ..."

And then he put the card back down, feeling for the first time like he was prying. Glancing over the other cards in this drawer, he saw that most of them were from this mysterious "*WB*". All of them, in fact, except for one; a postcard from George's parents, from their last holiday together as a family.

It wasn't useful, but he stared at it anyway.

From downstairs, a noise interrupted George's thoughts. It wasn't his imagination; footsteps were climbing the bottom staircase. He was stuck in here, *and he still hadn't found the evidence to confirm his suspicions*. Feeling desperate now, George reached down to the bottom drawer and pulled. It wouldn't budge at first, so he pulled harder. At last it slid open, but made a horrible scraping sound as it did. The footsteps below paused, just as George dragged the drawer out so quickly that the whole thing pulled out completely, spilling over the floor.

"No," George whimpered, and tried stupidly to stab the drawer back in, the footsteps climbing the second staircase now, getting closer all the time. After two attempts he gave up, lifted the drawer up and spilled it over the desk. A mess of papers fell out, and with condemned desperation, George grabbed at them and frantically began to read.

Subject: Re: Temporary Accommodation

Dear Zeedie,

Please, there's no need to thank me, you will be doing me a huge favour. I'm sorry I've been out of your life for so long. It's been hard, as you can imagine. Perhaps if I'd been around to help more with the business side of things . . .

But you don't need to hear that now! Instead, enjoy the house. You'll have no interruptions, no visitors at all until you're sure you've recovered from the breakdown. I'll make sure even the deliveries are discrete. If you could perform some maintenance on the house and gardens it would be totally appreciated. Also, perhaps keep it quiet that you're staying there? There's still ownership disputes that I'd rather not kick up . . .

Main thing is — you get some rest, and get recovered.

Your old friend,

W.B.

A shadow fell over the desk, and George looked up. A figure was there, thin and tall. But George did not shy away.

"This isn't your house," he said. "Is it, Uncle Zeedie?"

Chapter Twenty-Five

Just a few steps into the woods, and Lacey was getting lost. She hadn't taken this path before, hadn't been here at night without Rose either. It was far more confusing than she'd anticipated, made worse by a thickening mist that drifted in through the trees. But she didn't stop, didn't slow, driven on by the knowledge that George was alone with a murderer in the house.

"Rose?" she called out, and was greeted by stern silence. Was George right? Were there really no birds or other animals out here? Even the trees seemed to flee her phone torch, splayed out like a panicked and brutalised crowd. Losing her nerve, Lacey foolishly sped up, scratching her arms on the branches that she shoved aside, losing all sense of direction before running and ...

She hit something and sprawled, gasping, to the wet mulchy floor. Clinging to her composure, Lacey pulled herself back up using the thing she'd hit. It was soft, unpleasant to touch – and as she stood up, clumps of it fell away like a digestive biscuit. Still, enough remained. It was a sign, more complete than the last one she'd seen, and it stood in the middle of the path she'd lost.

BARKER HOMES
Elegant
Living

At once Lacey felt relieved. Rose's house must be nearby! Chuckling, she stepped closer to the sign and covered one part of it, then another.

"*Ega . . . ivin*," she said wryly. "And there I was thinking it was some ancient name for rocks. You lot were making fun out the townie."

Tracing the path ahead carefully with the torch, Lacey followed it as it wound uphill. Soon the path skirted alongside a tumbled-down fence, wrapped in vines.

"Jeez, Rose," Lacey said to herself. "Your manor needs a tidy up." And then she turned a corner, reached a clearing, and saw just how right she was.

The house was modern-looking; huge, American, and . . . crumbling. Like Uncle Zeedie's house the windows stretched tall and wide, but no light shone in any of the rooms. This was Rose's place? Where, then, was Rose? With growing urgency – *George, George, are you alright, George* – Lacey jogged up the path to the front door, reached for the heavily tarnished door knocker and . . .

The front door creaked open itself, its wood as rotten as the sign. Behind it was a house that had never been finished.

The wind blew through those big windows, completely devoid of glass. Vines were *growing* down the staircase, and as Lacey took a step forwards, the rotten floor groaned with such a withered agony that she stepped quickly back.

"Rose," Lacey whispered, stepping backwards. "Rose. Where... where..."

"Lacey," a voice said, and a cold hand touched the back of her neck.

"Jesus!" Lacey gasped, and whirled around... before wanting to cry with relief. "Rose!" she said, and without thinking threw her arms around her. "I thought this was your house!"

"No, silly!" Rose said with a smile. "Why are you even out here?"

"What is this place? Why are *you* even out here?"

"We spend time here, sometimes." Rose shrugged.

"Uncle Zeedie... you were *right*, Rose," Lacey said, and clenched her fists so that fingernails dug into her palms. "He's... the missing kids, those missing kids, oh god—"

"Lacey—"

"He killed them, Rose, and George is still there with him, oh god, George is there—"

"LACEY."

Lacey stopped, breathing hard, and looked at Rose. Here, in moonlight, the girl seemed older, possessed with an unearthly stillness, her skin pale and ice-cold, her eyes alert but completely, utterly calm. They soothed Lacey, those eyes.

"We need to be quick," said Rose. "There's a shortcut through the woods. Okay? We'll call the police, and get you and your brother safe."

Lacey nodded. It was so good to see her. "Okay. Let's go."

Chapter Twenty-Six

"Is it true?" George repeated the question, trying to be forceful although his voice was quavering. "This isn't your house?"

He understood now, what Lacey had said about Uncle Zeedie's anger. He didn't shout, but his eyes were baltic cold, his lips thin as a blade. He wasn't just angry, he was *furious*. Had George made a fatal mistake, staying here?

"I don't see why it's any concern of yours," Uncle Zeedie replied sternly, "or why you are in this office in the middle of the—"

"Because Lacey thinks you're a murderer!"

Uncle Zeedie paused. "What?"

George took a breath. All he could do was speak, and hope.

"We found all these *Missing Child* pamphlets around the house, even though you said you hadn't heard about the missing children near here."

"I *didn't* hear about any—"

"We found jewellery and toys belonging to the missing children too, in my bathroom and in the lockers in the pool changing rooms. You said you couldn't get into the basement, and Lacey found *four* keys to that door in your room."

"That *key*? I found a key in my chest of drawers this evening, I had never seen it—"

"*And* she found your clothes covered with blood in the wardrobe."

Uncle Zeedie paled. "That was as disturbing to me as it was to you—"

"And *then*, when she looked in the basement she found blood and . . . and cut-up flesh."

At that last word, Uncle Zeedie swayed. "How . . . why would . . ."

"Whose house is this, Uncle Zeedie?" George urged.

Uncle Zeedie stared at him, silent. For a long moment he loomed over the desk, shadowed and sinister, as though weighing up the manner of George's death. Then, carefully, as though he might collapse, he sat down.

"You are correct," he said weakly. "This house belongs to my friend. My best friend. We hadn't spoken for so long, years in fact, not since he'd lost his daughter. But then I lost my house. I lost *everything*."

"You mean, your business? It—"

"My business failed. I was bankrupt, everything I had worked for just . . . died. The shock of it, it left me . . . unwell, with nowhere to go. With nobody else to turn to, I contacted my old friend."

"And he helped."

"Amazingly, after years of silence, he did. He had made millions from building and selling houses, and he said he had a place for me to stay until I got back on my feet. It was in splendid isolation, he said. I wouldn't have to see another soul."

"And then we came to mess it up."

Uncle Zeedie sighed. "Precisely the opposite, George. I know I don't translate my... feelings well, but I was excited to hear of your visit. So excited that I didn't want your parents to know about my dire situation and cancel. I even worried about the state of this run-down house. I've kept working on it, in fact, at night, when you two were supposed to be asleep."

"So that's why you keep sneaking out at night?" said George. Was this believable? He couldn't decide. "So... what? Somebody's *framing* you as a murderer, snatching kids and making it look like you? If it's your friend, they must *hate* you."

"Not my friend," Uncle Zeedie said, "he's not a killer. If you'd seen him after his daughter died, you would know."

George sighed. His mind went back to earlier in the evening, his collapse in the living room. What he had seen and heard in that brief moment... neither Uncle Zeedie *nor* his friend could be the gruesome serial killer.

The trouble was, based on what the Feeling had shown him? *Nobody* could.

"Are you okay, George? You've gone quiet."

George nodded. He wasn't going to tell Uncle Zeedie about the Feeling, not until he could be sure to trust him. But to trust him, they'd have to go somewhere George *really* didn't want to go.

"We need to look in that basement," he said at last.

Chapter Twenty-Seven

"Eurgh," said Uncle Zeedie, and gagged again. "Sour milk. I've been trying to scrub away that smell for a week. It has come from here all this time?"

George didn't reply. He stretched his T-shirt over his nose, stepped slowly down the basement steps, and...

...and he saw the huge bloodstain across the concrete floor. The Feeling returned and George felt sick, a rush of heat and headache throbbing at his vision. He looked back to see Uncle Zeedie loom up behind him... and switched on his torch.

"Come on," he said tightly.

Grimacing, George crossed the concrete floor, skirting the bloodstain and still trying to keep an eye on his uncle, whose face looked more sinister than ever down here in the gloom. The basement was surprisingly small, empty save for the blood... and a gruesome little shrine to death at the far end. The *Missing Child* posters caught George's eye first, and for a wild moment he imagined Uncle Zeedie cackling in his high voice, as he ran across the basement towards him, manic bloody murder in his eyes.

"George?" Uncle Zeedie murmured from the bottom step. "Are you okay?"

Silently, George forced himself to take in the menagerie of murder; the dozens of posters, the stolen clothes and pickled limbs, the baskets of jewellery and decaying chunks of flesh. It was gruesome. It was evil. It . . .

"It feels fake," he murmured. "It feels staged."

"I did not do this," Uncle Zeedie whispered, and George glanced around at him. That strange, unsettling smirk still lingered on his uncle's face. For some people it would be a disturbing expression to see in anyone witnessing such horrors. But then, what kind of maniac sets their face for something like this?

Mind racing, George shone his torch around the shelves. He noticed another shelf, up high above the noticeboard, so high that it was just below the wooden floorboards of the level above. Stepping back, all the way back to the steps, George pointed his torch at the high shelf and saw what it was.

"That's where the smell is coming from," he murmured. All across the shelf, stood in an untidy row, were bottles of milk. They were all half full, their lids off, a thick mouldering gloop sat gently stewing inside them.

"I don't understand," Uncle Zeedie said. "Why would somebody want this house to smell of sour milk?"

"Maybe . . ." George murmured, "Maybe because the magazine said that's what serial killers smell like."

Just then, a tapping sound came from the wall behind

Uncle Zeedie. George turned, shining his torch first at his uncle, then at the wall.

"What?" Uncle Zeedie said. "What is it?"

"You didn't hear that?" George said, and again shone his torch at the wall. Too late, he realised what the tapping sound was. It was the sense of dread, the watery nausea at the back of his dry throat. It was the figure in the armchair, the doll in the plughole, the opening locker door.

It was the Feeling, and it hit him like a slap.

"George," Zeedie said, striding over as George doubled over. "Are you alright? What's happening?"

George couldn't respond. He retched, gasped at the migraine grinding into his skull like a dentist's drill. He fell to one knee, limbs seizing up, drool stringing from his mouth, one hand squeezing his forehead as if to stop his brains spurting out. It was dreadful, this Feeling – the worst it had ever been. The only respite was a cold, damp draught on his face.

A cold, damp draught.

"George, what is wrong?!" Uncle Zeedie exclaimed. George couldn't answer, but was recovering at last. Slowly, with his lungs full, eyes streaming, the Feeling began to fade, and George's vision cleared, enough that he could see something important.

A cold, damp draught.

The breeze was coming through a gap along the bottom of the wall. Caught in that gap was Lacey's magazine, *The Blood Texts*. It was on a different page than before, a different article to that silly questionnaire, and whether the page had been turned by ghostly hands or by good fortune, George would never know.

"George, tell me you're okay," Uncle Zeedie pleaded, "Oh, I can't see your parents letting you stay again after all this."

George saw his uncle try to pat his shoulder, then give up and pat the air instead. *Uncle Zeedie doesn't like to be touched*, George remembered, and smiled, even though he felt rough. Then he pulled out the magazine and clambered to his feet.

Chapter Twenty-Eight

"Rose," Lacey begged, "Rose, listen."

Her phone was dying. The woods were smothered in darkness and mist, the moon's pale light waning. Getting to the village had taken a long time before, but they'd walked this winding and claustrophobic dirt track for *hours*. Lacey's terror for her brother's safety had decayed into forlorn lost hope.

"I *have* to get to the village," she implored. "Rose, please, I – let's get back to the road. I don't think you know where this path goes. Rose, STOP!"

"We know every path in the Sink," Rose said, her voice flat. "We've walked them so many times."

At last the trees cleared, and the mists with them, quite suddenly exposing a wide clearing. Puzzled, Lacey made her way towards the centre of it. It was familiar somehow, and as she shone her torch around...

She let out a sob.

It was the place she had mistakenly called *Ega ivin*, the circle of six tall boulders Rose had brought her to the night before. All that walking, and they were barely one hundred metres from Uncle Zeedie's house. A terrible hurt wrenched at Lacey's heart, the crushing disappointment that a girl in whom she'd placed her last ounce of faith had led her along this exhausting wrong path.

"You tricked me." She said it with a choked voice, and her fists clenched as she did. "Why did you trick me? What is wrong with you? I have to help my brother!"

But Rose didn't turn around. Instead, she idly walked on, behind the tallest rock. Lacey strode across the circle towards her, ready to grab her, to rag her back and *scream*.

"What the... *Why* have we come here?! *Why* didn't we just take the road?!"

But with the whisper of moved air, Rose had vanished. Perplexed, Lacey stepped back and looked around. Rose was back in the middle of the circle, smiling an infuriating smile.

"Let me tell you about this place," said Rose, "and you'll understand why we're here."

THE VAMPYRE'S COUSIN: THE KAZLUK

"A clap of lightning, a trickle of blood meandering down the neck. And then the savage attack began; and naught was heard save a squeal, and the frenzied mauling of flesh."

That's an account of a vampire attack witnessed

by a French aristocrat travelling through what is now known as Croatia during the Thirteenth Century. Or was it? For another type of vampire exists that is barely known at all. The Kazluk.

Ancient the Kazluk may be, perhaps even as old as the caves in which they dwell. Human they may appear; indeed, many accounts have them able to speak. But they will never leave their cave. They will never grow, will never love, will never convert another to their kind, will never possess any goal beyond that of capturing and devouring their prey. If vampires are aristocrats, living in castles and drinking the blue blood of highborn maidens, the Kazluk are a pack of attack dogs with human faces.

1942, Croatia: a German shell lands in the Neretva Valley, exposing a series of caves. Allied troops discover 'sleeping' bodies in those caves, all without heartbeats, all apparently still breathing. Medical teams race in . . . but as the midday sun shines over the exposed bodies, they moulder and 'die' in a grim conflagration that leaves these grizzled veterans deeply shaken. 'Accidental Fire' is the official explanation given.

Beauty? Yes. Like vampires, the Kazluk are rumoured to possess the looks of eternal youth. But while the Kazluk do not age, nor do they multiply. Nobody knows how they arrived on this earth, but when the last Kazluk dies, no more shall take their place.

1865, Mississippi: A wealthy family vanishes entirely, their house 'painted with blood' according to one local rag. The chief suspect? A young man seen near the house. But the hunt provides some strange witness accounts.

"I'd never forget that face," one local vows. "When I was nine my sister asked that man to dance at County Fair, and we never saw her again." The local was sixty-five years old.

Creatures of the night? Mostly . . . Although stories indicate a violent reaction to direct sunlight, some rumoured Kazluk sightings have taken place during daytime. Perhaps an overcast day, or a heavily shaded area, is enough for them to survive. Other supposed weaknesses are also unproven. Garlic possesses no threat, and even religious artefacts have little evidence of success, as shown in the deeply unpleasant case of Father Bakari.

1984, Benin. In this largely rural West African state, Father Akambi Bakari maps a historical pattern of mysterious child deaths over decades. Six deaths, every seven years. At the centre of this map is a steep, almost craterous valley. Incanting every prayer, donning every cross and rosary, the brave Father Bakari blesses himself with holy water, and marches fearlessly down the pit.

They find his body on the road days later, mutilated beyond recognition. Written in the dirt

with a broken finger is the priest's final word: *Adze*. Vampire.

Though we pity the poor Father, he is mistaken. Kazluk, not vampires, hibernate for seven years, before waking to murder once more. Kazluk, not vampires, are deeply territorial, and will not leave the area they have inhabited since time began. If vampires are svelte seducers of myth, then Kazluk are the brutal killers of reality.

Chapter Twenty-Nine

"Vampires."

Uncle Zeedie had barely read the article before he repeated the word with a *very* condescending tone. So George ignored him.

"Can we open this?" he said instead, and he pushed at the wall. It didn't budge, so he aimed a kick at it.

"It's a wall, George. I don't know who is playing this cruel joke on me, but we will not get carried away with—"

CLUNK.

The sole of George's slipper was rubber – not heavy enough for the kick not to hurt his foot, but heavy enough to hear the echo as it bounced off the 'wall'. And the wall bounced too – not far, not even a foot. But it moved.

"I think this might be a door," George said.

Uncle Zeedie stared at it. His face was flat, expressionless, which George was starting to understand meant he was shocked.

"The police," he said quietly. "We should call the police."

"There's no signal," George reminded him. "And, Uncle

Zeedie, I don't know if this is the sort of thing the police can—"

"Well we'll walk up the hill, then."

"But if the magazine is right, then—"

"The magazine isn't right," Uncle Zeedie snapped, his voice hoarse. "It's not a rational thing, George. *The magazine isn't right!*"

George took a long breath. There was nothing else for it. He'd have to tell him everything.

"Do you know why I didn't run away with Lacey tonight?" he asked finally.

"Because you didn't suspect me of being a serial killer."

George nodded. "But why didn't I? Wouldn't you? If you'd seen and heard everything I'd seen, wouldn't you?"

Uncle Zeedie didn't answer.

"I suspected you up until this evening," George said honestly. "And then I saw something that didn't make sense. Something unbelievable."

George took a breath. And he spoke, very haltingly, about the Feeling. He told his uncle about the bodies hanging in the train station, and the voices in the middle of the night. He saw his uncle look at him with disbelief, at first, then pity. Then, as he talked about finding the doll's head in the drain, and the ring in the locker, he saw his uncle's face change to fear.

"You didn't see those things," his uncle insisted. "Think logically, George. You think you did, but you didn't."

"I don't think we were supposed to find them," George continued relentlessly. "I think they were for the police to find, after me and Lacey and maybe even you were dead. But they showed me to them, these ghosts. And when Lacey opened the basement door, they all flooded out, all at once." He took a slow, shuddering breath. "And there were loads of them, Uncle Zeedie, loads of kids. There were kids in old clothes, with old-fashioned faces, who spoke in old ways that I could barely understand. There was a girl in a stripey top, with braces on and big glasses. There were three boys, brothers I think, dressed in caps and woolly blazers like they were from wartime. There were—"

"The boys," Uncle Zeedie interrupted, "what did they say?"

"They all said the same thing. 'Those woods aren't safe.' Those *woods*, Uncle Zeedie. Not this house, not you. Those woods."

Uncle Zeedie wiped the sweat from his waxen brow. Down here, under torchlight, he looked uncannily like an android. A *broken* android.

"When my friend first offered me this house," he said at last, "I looked the area up online. There were many missing-children cases, a surprising number, but then who knows what *is* a surprising number? And then there was a historical article. It was about three boys, triplets, who'd stayed with a local family during the war. They were from quite a well-to-do family in London, and when they vanished it caused public outrage. The foster parents were charged but never prosecuted, and the one quote I could find from the father made me remember the case. 'I told them not to go to the Sink,' he said."

Zeedie broke off. He still looked doubtful.

"But then, *you* could have researched this. You might have seen the story somewhere. Or you and your sister came up with this whole joke."

"You'll never completely believe me," said George. "I get it. *I* wouldn't believe me – like you wouldn't believe you. But with all those dead kids in front of me, tens, *hundreds* of them . . . I mean, it couldn't be you, could it? It couldn't be your friend even, not unless he is impossibly old. And as unbelievable as that article seems, if it's true then Lacey is in danger, and it's not from anything the police would believe in. So *please*, Uncle Zeedie. *Please* can you move this wall."

Uncle Zeedie stared at him, speechless. Then, finally, he shoved into the wall and began to push. George joined him. After a moment, the wall – or door – at last began to open. It didn't squeak, it was just very heavy, a thick frame sitting on wheels, and once it started to move, those wheels sped up. George and Zeedie pushed with all their strength, one step at a time . . . until the heavy door was wide open.

Behind it was a tunnel, small and completely pitch black, an abyss utterly without light. George shone his phone torch in, revealing walls of earth and clay, dug barely high enough for him to stand, and nothing else. It was a tunnel from ancient days, a tunnel dug by hands.

He glanced at Uncle Zeedie and said, "C'mon."

One word, but it sounded brave – *much* braver than he felt. Then, before he could chicken out, George walked into the tunnel first. After a moment, Uncle Zeedie followed.

— Chapter Thirty —

"Long ago, this place used to be called the *bendigaill*," Rose said quietly. "People used to come here to worship. Long ago."

"We've got to help George. *Now*." Lacey meant to sound commanding. She didn't.

"A tribe lived at the base of the Sink, you see. They were wise, this tribe. Every seven years, they would give six of their village, leave them at this place to die. It was a tribute they paid to a higher order of beings."

"Rose..." Lacey pleaded. "We need to *go*." She turned to leave herself, to chance the dark and race for the top of the hill. But then she froze.

Something had moved. There, behind the tallest rock of the circle.

"But humans are greedy," Rose continued, her voice dreamlike. "They spread like disease. They forget their true place, of *cig noeth*. They no longer wish to pay tribute to their masters."

"There's something there..." Lacey murmured, staring at the tall, vine-draped boulder.

"This human tribe, the day came where they thought up a cunning deceit, a devilish trick. They would turn day into night.

"As their masters slept, they pushed and pruned and persuaded the surrounding trees to grow apart. Then, when there was nothing above these boulders but sky and stars, they wove a liar's canopy, a giant's blanket of branches, so thick, so magnificent, that it blocked the light from the sky. And when their masters awoke, they saw nothing but darkness and the tribute that they expected; six children, seated patiently in the *bendigaill*."

"Wait . . ." Lacey said, and turned to Rose with a frown. "Wait – these things ate *children*?"

"Their masters did not pause for a moment," Rose said. "Oh no. They hurried to their gift, for the moment they awoke was always when their hunger was greatest." Rose stared grimly up at the exposed sky. "And then, as the masters feasted, the people pulled their canopy back . . . and let the sunlight in."

". . . Vampires," said Lacey. Now Rose faced her, and the hate on her face sent chills down her spine.

"But, you see, the people made a mistake. They pulled their trick too soon. Three of their masters escaped! Thinking they had won a great battle, this tribe ran back to their village at the base of this valley, congratulating themselves for their great courage, their mighty cunning. Only later, many hours later, when their last begging wench was choking on their own blood, did they truly understand the terrible mistake they had made. For this is *our* land."

Lacey stared at Rose, disturbed by her tale. Then urgency snapped her to her senses.

"I've had enough of this, I'm *going*—"

The vines covering the headless statue pulled back to reveal Rose's friend, Kendra.

"*Rose, we've got to go,*" she mimicked. "*Rose, we've got to go.*"

Her laugh was high and cruel.

Chapter Thirty-One

The tunnel was damp and warm, and far from even. It shrunk in places, so tight that George was forced to crawl, squeezing between rocks that bruised and jarred his body. Elsewhere it widened, enough to *almost* stand but never quite, meaning that soon George's neck ached horribly. Some points were alarmingly soft, and when George made the mistake of resting against a tunnel wall, soil broke away and poured over him in a miniature collapse. With a blinding terror of being buried alive, he ran forwards only for the tunnel to shrink again, beneath thick rock that raked his scalp and forced him down with a hot, wet pain pulsing through his skull.

"George?" Uncle Zeedie's pale voice trembled through the dark behind him. "George? George!"

George craned around, and his heart sank. He'd never had to be the calming presence before, but Uncle Zeedie looked utterly petrified, his every limb sharp and angular, like a paper-mâché model that would crumple any minute now.

"I should probably choose this moment to tell you that

I'm very scared of enclosed spaces," he said.

"It's, er, it's okay, Uncle Zeedie," George replied. "I don't think we're far away now."

"How do you know?" Uncle Zeedie still didn't move, his breathing shallow and panicked.

"Well . . ." George shone his torch onwards. It showed darkness, going on seemingly for ever. "I'm sure it can't be that far."

Uncle Zeedie nodded, but still he didn't move. He tried to move one hand . . . and it trembled. He shook his head, and the hand clamped back into earth.

This was bad. If they did exist, these Kazluks, what if one came for a stroll down here? *Move!* George silently urged Uncle Zeedie. *Please move!* But his uncle couldn't.

And then the Feeling returned.

"No," he groaned, and bowed his head.

"George? Are *you* oka—"

It took George a moment to wonder why his Uncle had broken off. When he did, he looked up. And he saw the glowing light.

It wasn't bright. It was cold, and blue, and weak . . . but it *was* there. It shone from lamps and lanterns, torches and tealights. The hands that held them were all sizes, but none had seen adulthood, none ever would. The children kept their heads bowed, their eyes cast down as they stepped into the tunnel just ahead of George, forming a silent procession onwards and away. That pale-blue luminescence illuminated the path they took, and the tunnel was not so dark any more.

"That . . ." Uncle Zeedie breathed, and looked to George with a terrified, flabbergasted amazement. "You . . ." he said. He couldn't manage any more.

"I think we have to follow them, Uncle Zeeds," George said. "Let's go now."

He sounded like his big sister, he realised.

Chapter Thirty-Two

Lacey had been at a house party once, ages ago, and her friend's boyfriend had turned up. He'd joked around a lot, and they'd all thought he was amazing because he had a car and loads of money, but something about his careful, predatory eyes had made Lacey think, *You're too old to hang out with us.*

Now she stepped backwards across the stone circle, the threat of violence hanging heavy in the mist. She looked from face to face at three people she had previously thought might become her friends: Rose, Kendra and River. And again she thought of that house party, of her friend's boyfriend, because their eyes seemed old and cruel, and Lacey felt impossibly young compared to them all.

"What's going on?" she said, smiling in fear. "That's a cool hiding spot, Kendra. Bit old to be playing in dens though, aren't we?"

River took a step towards her. There was menace in his gaze and Lacey didn't hesitate: she swung a fist at him, but he grabbed it and shoved her backwards. Not just shoved – Lacey was sent sprawling painfully to the wet forest floor.

"She wants to fight!" Kendra said, and let out a sharp, hyena-like laugh. Lacey struggled to her knees, spitting out wet leaves and dirt.

"Rose," she croaked. "Why are you doing this?"

"Why?" Rose said, her voice harsh. "You are tribute! There is nothing better you can be than tribute!" Her words were changing, Lacey noticed. Not the words themselves, but the way she spoke them. It was getting harder to understand her, like her lips were turning to rubber.

"What do you mean, tribute? Don't tell me you believe that stupid story you told."

"We don't just believe it, *cig noeth*," River growled – his voice also had that squashed sound, even more so than Rose. "We lived it."

Lacey scoffed, but there was something seriously wrong here. Rose's smile looked too big for her mouth, and Kendra was giggling constantly, in a way that seemed unhinged. For the first time since she'd left the house, Lacey began to feel that deep rancid chill; the dreadful sensation that comes with a genuine fear for your life.

"I'll be missed, you know," she warned. "If you do anything. My parents are coming to get me, and my Uncle Zeedie—"

"No," Rose said. Her jaw opened wide on the word, too wide, and there was something else behind her teeth. Lacey wondered if she was hallucinating. "No. The man promised us. He keeps his promises. He says all will be fine."

"Who? What man?"

"The Rich Man. He fixes things."

She wasn't hallucinating, Lacey realised. Their jaws were getting . . . wider. Every time Rose opened her mouth to speak, it opened *more*. Every time Kendra laughed that horrible laugh, her bottom jaw hung lower.

Lacey turned to see River approaching, and his mouth was *inhumanly* wide. She stared, utterly aghast, and then she saw with a sickening swoop of her stomach that *another set of teeth* sat in his mouth. They were small and sharp, these other jaws, every tooth pointed into triangles.

"What are you?" she said faintly.

"Hungry," said Rose, her words distorted by that gaping mouth. She pulled back her head in a wide, feral smile, like an animal about to bite out. "Hungry for *cig noeth*."

"*Cig noeth*," River crowed. "That's what you are. *Raw flesh*."

Chapter Thirty-Three

With the eerie glow of the dead's lanterns guiding them, the tunnel was easier to navigate. George kept on, still murmuring encouragement to Uncle Zeedie. Finally, after what felt like hours but wasn't, the ceiling rose into cracked crystalline rock and the ground dried into a fine grey sand. The blue lights floated away into the ether; no ghostly goodbye, no wish for luck. And still George's head pounded, still his stomach churned. If the Feeling he suffered could be described as a sensitivity to death, then here, death was everywhere.

They were in a huge underground chamber, so vast that the sound echoed and the opposite wall was fogged. At least it was lit; dim camping lights placed haphazardly by slime-glistened walls. Looking around, George heard a noise ahead and dipped his phone torch.

"There's someone here," he whispered. Sure enough, at the opposite side of the cavern, a whole football pitch away, somebody was moving around, talking loudly as they did. George looked to Uncle Zeedie for guidance, got none, and crept forwards anyway.

It was foul, this cavern. It smelled of raw meat and waste. The floor was as filthy as cat litter, and twice George's thin rubber slipper sole smeared on something that stank. Thin, grim husks lay strewn like empty sacks, and small, tooth-sized pebbles peppered the sandy ground. Huge towering columns stood here and there. George thought they were gigantic stalagmites until he took a closer look.

He soon regretted it. These towers weren't towers, they were *heaps*; enormous piles of discarded toys and clothes, a morbid museum of childhood, clumped and festered into these gigantic pillars. Some of the possessions were disturbingly new – a shiny key fob here, half a branded trainer there. Others were so decayed George could barely tell what they were; wisps of lace, faded plastic, an ancient book with a teddy bear etched into the hardback cover and washed-out mush where the pages should be. It was everything the Kazluk had snatched from their victims, tossed without thought till the pile reached too high and they'd begun a new garbage tip elsewhere. Only through sheer willpower did George keep the awful sight from overwhelming him. Then his torchlight caught the headless body of a mermaid Barbie doll, and he let out a low moan.

"They're monsters," Uncle Zeedie whispered. People who didn't know him would've wondered why he smirked. But George heard the tremor in his voice, and caught the white-hot fury in that serrated smile. "They've got to be stopped."

And they turned to the figure chattering at the far wall.

Moving ahead, Uncle Zeedie cut diagonally across the

cave with a surprising speed, darting from mound to mound, until they reached the final mountain of toys, and peered out.

The far wall of the cavern was lined with shelves. A pallet truck with big tyres and stacked with food crates sat nearby. The figure was taking tins of food out of the crates, talking as he did. He was still turned away, but this close George could see and hear that he was an old man.

"I got the tinned peaches you like anyway, Izzy," he said. "They didn't have the fruit salad, but beggars can't be choosers, can we?"

Whoever this Izzy was, she didn't answer, but the man chuckled anyway, a chuckle that turned into a violent, hacking cough. George had heard that cough before – but before he could place it, Uncle Zeedie nudged him. He was looking in the opposite direction, to the far corner of the cavern, where a stack of metal boxes were dimly lit by a hole in the ceiling far above. That hole, George realised, was the source of the breeze that blew all the way through to the basement.

"Look at the boxes," Uncle Zeedie whispered. "*Star-Brite Remote Controlled Fireworks*. Whichever idiot brought them down here left the box of ignitors on top."

"Ignitors?" asked George.

"The things that make them go boom."

He was right. On top of the metal crates, there was another, cardboard box marked *25-Metre Ignitor – Pre-Paired With Star-Brite Remote Controlled Fireworks: Just Place And Press!*

"Why would anybody even want fireworks down here?" George asked.

Uncle Zeedie shook his head. His gaze shifted to the old man. He was still unloading the tins onto the metal shelves, and he must've been doing this for a long time, because there were *loads* of metal shelves, all stacked with food and stretching off into the distance.

"Look at all those supplies. There's enough to last years. Maybe . . . maybe they want to seal the entrances. A small explosion, just enough to block any access. Then they wait down here for seven years. Isn't that how long the magazine said these Kazluk hibernate?"

"Would that even work?"

"Maybe. It's a dangerous plan, given how unstable that tunnel was. It sounds more intricate than something the Kazluk themselves would come up with too, at least the way that magazine made them sound. Is this man even one of them? He seems old and . . ."

The figure turned, just enough for the light filtering down through the hole to catch his face. At once George recognised him.

"It's the delivery driver we met," he whispered. "The one who warned us at the shop, warned us about you, Uncle Zeedie! His name is Bill . . ."

George trailed off. Uncle Zeedie's face was a mannequin of shock, his eyes bulging, his mouth open. It was the most emotional he had ever seen him.

"It can't be," he murmured. "It . . . *no*."

And he stepped out.

"*Uncle Zeedie!*" George hissed, but it was no good.

Still oblivious, Bill kept unpacking the food crate, nattering away.

"I'll admit, I overdid it on the tinned spinach, Iz. Used to always be the thing in cartoons when I was little, good source of iron and—"

"William," Uncle Zeedie said. His friend stopped his chatter and turned around. *William*, George thought, *WB. It's his friend, the owner of the house!*

For a long moment the two men stared at each other. Then, as if nothing out of the ordinary had happened, William turned back around, and kept moving the tins.

"Uncle Zeedie's here, Iz. It's okay, my sweet, he won't be staying long."

Chapter Thirty-Four

Lacey was going to die here, she knew. Her three 'friends' approached her, hunger in their eyes, those small protruding teeth ever-grinning. Shaking with fear, she crab-walked backwards through the dirt, until River stomped one foot as if attacking, and she collapsed.

Distract them, her mind screamed. *Delay them.*

"So all that stuff you said about Death House, about my Uncle Zeedie," she said. "That was all a lie?"

"Rrrich Man 'old us to ssay that, 'irl," Rose growled softly. Her voice was becoming more distorted by her dangling mouth, though not as much as her friends'.

"*Iht keaps us' ayfe,*" River added, barely able to sound the words. Lacey had no idea what he said or who the "Rich Man" was. But she had to stall them.

"The Rich Man?" she said, trying to sound scornful. "The Rich Man's lying to you."

"Sssshe *'ant's a IGHT*!" Kendra said, with an insane, eye-rolling grin. *She wants a FIGHT!* But River and Rose had slowed. They exchanged a look. When Rose turned back, those jaws stretched wider than ever, those disturbing tiny teeth protruded further than before and she uttered one, distorted word from the back of her throat.

"*Speak*."

Lacey thought fast. Who was this "Rich Man"? How could she convince these . . . things that he actually meant to harm them? What did they care about, and what would they view as a threat? Then she remembered the end of Rose's story. *This land is ours*. Whoever had built the luxury houses in this valley hadn't cared, perhaps hadn't even known, that they were building on "Rose's land".

"This – this whole valley, it's going to be cut down," she said quickly. "People are coming with bulldozers and – and chainsaws and – they're building more houses. Loads of houses. There's *millions* of people out there without houses! They're going to move in here and this . . . this Rich Man just wants to distract you. He builds houses, look, with his company, Elegant Living. *Egan Ivin*, look, that's part of his sign, that's your *Rich Man's* company! He knows that you would fight for this land. If he can blame you for all the missing children, he won't *need* to stop you. The police will come, the army too, probably. You won't beat all of them."

Lacey came to an abrupt halt, breathing hard. She stared into the eyes of the creature she'd called Rose. A glimmer of doubt gave her hope. Had she gotten lucky about this "Rich Man"? Could Elegant Living actually be his company?

"*Nhe gol?*" said River. It was a question, but his vowels were so stretched by those widening jaws that Lacey couldn't understand. He repeated the question, "*Nhe gol?*" and Lacey thought, *gol, gol, grl, girl* ...

"The girl?" she asked. River nodded, and for a brief moment she felt a burst of relief ... before realising that she didn't know who 'the girl' was.

"The girl too," she said uncertainly. "She'll be locked up. You'll all be blamed. They'll bulldoze this whole area, and you'll all be locked up."

For a moment, she thought it had worked. River and Kendra looked to one another. Their jaws hung lower now, attached only by skin, those small, pointy teeth jutting straight out between them. When suddenly a grating, sawdust sound scratched from their throats, Lacey wondered what it meant. Then she realised they were laughing.

"Sssshe lies!" Kendra exclaimed, and she and River laughed some more, behind cruel, cold, aged eyes. Only Rose remained still, head pointed slightly down, eyes pointed slightly up, feral as they regarded Lacey's terror.

"No, really," Lacey lied desperately. "They—"

And Rose leapt for her throat.

Chapter Thirty-Five

"William . . . why?" Uncle Zeedie said, his voice higher than ever. "What made you . . ."

Uncle Zeedie stopped short then, staring down at something. Still behind the mountain of toys, George peered out . . . and saw it. Or rather, her. Lying on a large, flat slab of rock was a girl who could've been asleep. George recognised her from the photograph he'd found in Uncle Zeedie's desk drawer. She was William's daughter, Isabella.

"Oh, Will," Uncle Zeedie said.

"Don't 'Oh, Will' me," William snapped. "You're no good at emotion, Zeedie, you know that. I'm saving my daughter's life. When Izzy wakes up—"

"Is that what you are hoping to achieve here? You want her to wake as one of these . . . these creatures? Because she won't. *The Blood Texts* says the Kazluk cannot convert or multiply. They just exist. When the last Kazluk dies, they will be no more. Which is a *good* thing," Uncle Zeedie said. "How could you even imagine your daughter as one of them?"

"They are the oldest people on Earth," Will retorted. "Its original inhabitants."

"They're savage murderers."

"Now you sound like that bigoted magazine."

"*Children*, William. You are helping murderers take *children*."

"*I had to!*" Will hissed. "When I came back here and found a chance that my girl might be alive, I ..."

His voice trembled, and he broke off. In the silence that followed, George looked around, scouring the high cavern for an escape route. But there was only the tunnel they'd come through, and that small hole in the ceiling high above. He heard voices coming from that hole; rasping, distorted voices. The Kazluk, it had to be.

"I was so arrogant, Zeedie," William continued. "This ancient part of the world, with older secrets than our tiny heads could ever comprehend ... and what did I see? A luxury resort, where rich idiots like me and you could holiday for a few days every year. All my plans for the valley – holiday homes, boutique shops ... and then Izzy went missing, and they went out of the window. But her disappearance never made sense. And then I came across that magazine."

"*The Blood Texts*. You saw the article about the Kazluk."

Will chuckled. "At first I thought it was ridiculous. 'The Vampyre's Cousin'?! But I was so desperate, and it chimed with Izzy's disappearance. The number of missing-children cases around here is off the charts, and they spike *every seven years*. Likewise, the nearest village has held a folk dance *every seven years* since time immemorial, the memory of why lost for generations. Local myths warn you not to linger in the sink for too long because of some ancient threat. When I looked at the surveyor's report for the first house, *your* house for these past months, it even mentioned an old tunnel leading from the foundations, although it was dismissed as a natural geological phenomenon. It was wishful thinking, but I had to look. And then I found this cave."

"It must have been terrible."

"It was," said William, "And I was prepared to kill them all. My god, such hatred I felt! And then I found one victim left alive. They keep one alive for when they wake up. And it was my Isabella!"

George didn't hear Zeedie's response to this. He'd suddenly had an idea. A stupid, dangerous idea that might take out the Kazluk above them, and might blow him up along with Uncle Zeedie too. It was a huge risk, but with the mountains of toys behind him, all the litter from a thousand-year killing spree, it didn't seem like a hard choice to make at all. He peered out to William, waiting for him to turn away. But the sickly old man was still talking.

"Of course, my first idea was to grab Izzy. I tried to wake her and flee, but it was a mistake. She wasn't the same girl any more. I know that magazine says these 'vampires' cannot convert people into their own kind, but seeing her, I became certain they could. Whatever they do to their final prey in order to keep them alive for seven years, it could eventually transform that prey into Kazluk. These magnificent beings may never have *thought* to convert a human before . . . but that doesn't mean they can't."

"So you saw another life for your daughter," Uncle Zeedie said dryly.

"I did. Of course, I would first have to survive, because the Kazluk themselves had woken now. My god, they're so *strong*, they are killing machines! They hurt me, very deeply. Eventually, I think, I will die from the injuries they caused. But now I had a deal to offer them."

"A deal."

"Yes. You see, there are simply too many missing-children cases in this area for the Kazluk to remain unnoticed. The police have been slow to connect these cases, but it is only a matter of time before their investigations lead them to the Sink. Should that happen, these creatures will surely be discovered. They aren't just out of their time, they're out of their *epoch*. But, if I could hide them, and if somebody *else* could be blamed . . ."

"A scapegoat," Zeedie's voice was ice, "for all those dead children."

"I didn't want it to be you, Zeeds, you must believe that. I couldn't *ask* anyone to stay here. It would undermine the whole plan. I'd need someone to willingly hide out in that house. Somebody desperate for isolation. Somebody who – please forgive me – had that special secret sauce, whose very mannerisms can aggravate people. Somebody who is always thought of as *off*. I'd need a likely suspect. And yes, that likely suspect was you."

At last, William – or Bill, as George had known him – turned away to open another crate. George didn't delay. He turned and shot out silently across the sand, crouching beside the stack of fireworks. The pictures on the cardboard ignitor box showed just three steps.

REMOVE THE PLASTIC TAG FROM THE IGNITOR.
PRIME THE ROCKET BY PRISING OPEN THE TAIL.
PRESS THE BUTTON ON THE IGNITOR.

He could do that. As quietly as possible, George began to rip the cardboard box.

"I know it's wrong, Zeeds," William was saying, "*Beyond* wrong. I would've chosen *anyone* else, but when you contacted me I had no choice. It was nearly time for the Kazluk to feed again. They're not stupid. I'd told them about closing the entrance to this cave, and about finding a scapegoat. If I didn't have the scapegoat, they would have just killed me and Izzy."

"Plus, you now had two more children for them to eat."

"No, no," William said, raising his voice. "I didn't *ever* want that. I knew how much those kids meant to you, and when I saw them arrive, it . . . I was ready to abandon the whole plan right then, honestly I was. But then . . . I mean, that magazine is foul, but it mapped out quite the murderer, I'll admit. From the sour-milk smell, to the mouldy food, to the pamphlets dotted around the house, I had followed every step, and it was working. Your godchildren had begun to suspect you themselves . . ."

George had a strip ripped from the cardboard now. He peered into the box. The ignitors were sitting loose inside. He reached in and got his fingers round an ignitor, but when he pulled it another one fell out noisily. George froze, still visible. Fortunately, William hadn't noticed.

". . . even brought elements of my plan forward. I snuck into the house, daubed your clothes with blood and hid the basement keys in your room, enough of them for your godchildren to find if they followed my advice at he shop."

"Very clever," Uncle Zeedie said. "So they might send messages to their parents about me before your creatures killed them, was that why?"

"No," William insisted, "No, I didn't want to kill them, Zeedie, I—"

"Don't *lie*!" Uncle Zeedie snapped. "Of course they'd have to die! They're the final piece of the puzzle, the horror that the police find when they break through the door of this evil serial killer called Zeedie. You were going to let the Kazluk kill them, and then display their bodies after they'd killed me, so *stop lying*!"

He was angrier than George had ever seen him. And with William taken aback by this burst of rage, it was a good opportunity. George pulled the plastic tag from the ignitor, then, storing it in his hoodie pocket, he looked through the containers holding the fireworks. They were kept in metal tins, clasped tightly. There was no other way. He'd have to open one.

"Zeedie, it's for my daughter," William was begging quietly. "You've got to understand that—"

"I do *not* understand," Zeedie said emphatically. "This is an evil crime, committed for a plan that won't work. Izzy *won't* be converted. The police *will* uncover the truth. And your last thought before you die will be that you helped these monsters kill children."

There was silence, for so long that George looked up, his fingers on the metal clasp of the fireworks box. William was glaring at Uncle Zeedie, his hands hidden beneath the plastic food crate. Up until now he'd been charming and polite. Now he looked cornered, a cold, callous glare in his eyes. Suddenly George could see how this genial, gentle-sounding man could have done such terrible things.

"You always were an idiot, you know that, Zeeds?" William said softly. "The Weirdo, that's what we'd call you. We used to have this ongoing joke – every time you went on a date or had an interview, we would write down all the stupid stuff we thought you'd come out with. It's funny, our other nickname for you was The Serial Killer."

William took his hands out of the crate, and Uncle Zeedie took a step back. The older man was holding a gun. It was pointed at Uncle Zeedie, and George knew; it was now or never. No longer caring to be quiet, he gripped the metal clasp of the closest firework, and undid it. The lid opened with a loud, metallic, creak.

"What was that?" said William.

It all happened at once. Uncle Zeedie launched himself

at William, knocking the gun from his hand, and the two began to tussle. George grabbed the rocket out of the container, prised open its tail, and shoved it back in the box, praying it would be enough. As George ran, the two men fought on the floor, a messy fight, haphazard and rough. George dashed behind the mountain of toys, and peered round just in time to see Uncle Zeedie fling William to the floor and stagger back to his feet. But William grabbed the gun, aimed it and ...

"WILLIAM!" George shouted. The old man fired ...

... and missed, his eyes wide at the ignitor in George's hand.

"Your daughter would *hate* you," George seethed. "She would be so miserable. She would want you *dead*."

And he hit the button.

Chapter Thirty-Six

"NO!" Lacey screamed, and she punched and kicked, but it was no good. Rose's hands were incredibly strong, forming bruises every time she gripped her flailing limbs. The girl, the *creature*, crouched down into Lacey's neck, and instantly Rose felt those little teeth piercing her throat; not a sharp pain but a numbing sensation that was so much worse, that of her windpipe being pulled from her flesh.

Gagging, contorted, she grabbed at Rose's hair and twisted it as hard as she could, but it did nothing, and as Lacey felt something *give* in her throat she looked up to see Kendra and River approaching, those horrible jaws hanging freely, their teeth jutting forwards as–

"WILLIAM!"

The shout was muffled, somewhere *below*, and Lacey could've sworn it was George's voice. Rose paused, pulled back, her mouth coated with blood, and that awful, flesh-tearing sensation eased on Lacey's throat. Kendra, Rose and River looked at one another, uncertain. And then, just as River turned and ran towards the rock, there was a *WHOOMPH*.

And the rock disappeared.

It happened so quickly that Lacey understood nothing except to tumble back and away, clutching at her throat, gulping down sweet air. The ground was opening up behind her, the sounds of ongoing explosions pounding the collapsing earth from underneath. Lacey burst to her feet, arms windmilling up the tumbling avalanche of dirt, leaping and rolling and scrabbling up in a frenzied effort to escape the sinkhole. Down went the earth, down went the *Egan ivin* sign, down went the ancient rocks. For one moment Lacey was going down with them, for a moment her feet weren't fast enough, and...

With one last push she flung herself up, arms flailing, and by some miracle her fingers clutched to the branch of a tumble-down tree. There was a rush beneath her, clods of earth pouring into nothingness, threatening to drag her with it.

Then, incredibly, the rumble moved away.

Lacey stumbled up to solid ground, turned, and fell to the floor. Ears ringing, vision blurred, neck in *agony*, she coughed out brown spit and took in the devastation behind her. The sinkhole was *huge*, a dry swamp of cracked and broken rocks across the entire clearing. A sudden surge of sorrow threatened to sweep her away all over again.

George, she thought. Was that his voice? Was he down there?

But then she saw two figures clambering swiftly up the sunken rocks and forgot everything.

It was Kendra and Rose.

Without a breath's hesitation, Lacey clambered to her feet and *ran*, stumbling through the thickening trees, no idea of direction beyond forwards. More terrible cracks rumbled to her right, and she saw it. The ground hadn't stopped collapsing; it was trembling and weaving a path down the hill, like a finger dragged across an Etch A Sketch.

George, Lacey thought again, and felt a horrible certainty that he was somewhere beneath all that churning rubble. Without a plan she chased the collapsing ground, branches whipping her face until ...

At last, the path! And not just the path, but the bottom of it. Lacey turned a sharp left and burst out of the woods, racing past the hedge animals as somewhere behind her one of the Kazluk let out a dreadful high-pitched roar. Night was almost over, the pale promise of dawn casting a grey pallor over the valley. She had overtaken the slow rumble of collapsing earth, but it was right behind, and as Lacey reached the back door of Zeedie's house she glanced back to see the hedge animals topple over, swallowed by the roiling dirt. Then, just as she wondered if the entire house would collapse, the rumbling slowed and stopped. The collapse had reached the house's concrete foundations and had finally ceased.

And up the hill above it, two figures were pelting out of the woods at an inhuman speed towards her.

Lacey slammed the door handle open and burst into the hallway, heart in mouth.

"GEORGE!" she shouted, but a suffocating tsunami

of dust and dirt was gushing out from the open basement door, and Lacey knew that there was no way he could have survived it. "No," she sobbed, choking on the thick dirt air. "No. GEORGE!"

Somehow, she knew it. Her brother, her uncle. They'd been down there. They'd been crushed.

Lacey had never felt such loathing in her life. The thought that she had been tricked by the beast that Rose turned out to be left an sour, bitter, burning taste in her throat. With dust clouds pouring through the hallway, clogging her lungs, she turned and ran up the stairs. She had thought of a way to kill the creatures. She was going to copy the people from thousands of years before.

A liar's canopy, Rose had called it.

At the foot of the stairs, Lacey glanced across to the back door. Rose and Kendra were halfway down the hill. She had never seen anyone move so fast; leaping bushes and across boulders without breaking stride.

Good. Let them follow.

She ran up the stairs two at a time, then the same up the spiral stairs to the second floor. Not even halfway up there was a *CRACK!* that echoed violently through the house, something slamming into the back door with obscene force. Lacey heard the tearing sound of strengthened glass fracturing, then with another *CRACK!* the glass shattered, followed immediately by racing footsteps.

Lacey hurtled up to the second floor and grabbed the blue cord dangling down from the ceiling. She pulled at it –

nothing – then yanked it down with all her strength. Suddenly the hatch fell open, sending her sprawling as the heavy ladder slid down after it, barely missing her. Lacey leapt to her feet and was about to climb...

When the office door behind her slid open.

Chapter Thirty-Seven

Minutes earlier...

The explosion of fireworks in the cavern was quicker and more violent than George could have imagined. It didn't stop either – one almighty *BOOM* would cause four more, then ten more, then—

George turned to run, looked back to see Uncle Zeedie doing the same. He caught a glimpse of William by the wall behind them, lunging to put his arms protectively over his daughter, staring with utter dismay at the explosions careening towards him. George ran past the next mountain of toys, lost sight of William and Izzy, caught one last glimpse of the beautiful conflagration as it tore through the rock wall and...

For a second there was nothing but the ringing in his ears and the muffled sound of his own breath. There was silence, there was shock...

Then the ceiling collapsed.

It was the mountain of toys that saved him. The rocky ceiling smashed down on it with an almighty *whoomph*, sending dust clouds billowing through the cave. For a moment

George was utterly lost, drowning in a foul mist that poured gleefully into his lungs. Then a figure slammed into him.

"This way, George." It was Uncle Zeedie.

They ran. His vision clearing, George followed his uncle from tower to tower, using the brief shelter they provided before the monumental weight of falling earth and rock brought them tumbling down. Faster they ran, neither of them fast enough, and as George heard a snarl behind him, all his hope was lost.

It was the boy he'd seen on the drive here, the jawless boy with the backwards cap and torn jeans – the boy he'd once thought, on that first day, was a screaming ghost. He had been wrong. Close up, George could see that the boy wasn't screaming. His mouth was utterly slack, dangling from his face, and in the middle of the chasm it left were sharp and tiny teeth, a deadly and grotesque smile that was aimed at him. George had wanted to collapse this cave and bury the Kazluk with it. In his haste to see the plan through, he hadn't thought through the prospect of him being buried with them.

"Run, George!" Uncle Zeedie yelled, but he was *still* too slow, and the boy was toying with him now, was right behind him and about to swipe—

The Feeling hit George the moment they entered the tunnel, stronger than ever, an almighty migraine that made him cry out with pain. As it did, the same pale-blue light that led them here began to shine, but this time it intensified, becoming brighter and brighter until the whole tunnel glowed a blinding white. There was the sizzle of burning flesh, and the jawless boy screamed in pain, falling back. But the Kazluk was not done yet, and with the tunnel shrinking, with the thundering crash of falling rocks growing ever closer, it seemed that both George and Zeedie were doomed. Still they ran, soil pouring from every wall. Still they ran, breath tight against choking dust. Still they ran, catching deep gashes from plunging rocks, slipping on the dirt of a millennium's worth of corpses.

"*Cig NOETH!*" The roar came up behind George at a frightening pace. Something sharp swiped at the back of his neck, and hot liquid trickled out. Blind panic gripped him and he sped up, faster than he'd ever run in his life; so fast that he was dragging Uncle Zeedie behind him, their hands clenched into a white-knuckled claw. One more burst, and there it was; the basement, just ahead of them.

The distance was too far, of course it was. They couldn't make this, not with the earth collapsing and the Kazluk just behind, not when all fell apart. A second swipe sliced through George's shoulder; a flurry of rocks smashed into his skull. A foot swiped his legs out from under him and he smashed through the dirt, his hand losing Uncle Zeedie's, the momentum rolling him out of the tunnel and across the concrete floor with a bone-cracking violence.

The *concrete* floor. He'd made the basement.

Gasping, heaving, George hefted himself to his feet, his tears of pain drying into salt streaks before they could fall.

"Uncle Zeedie!" he coughed out the words, but there was no response. His hands shaking horribly, he took his phone from his pocket, and shone it back into the tunnel behind.

There were nothing but clouds of dust.

Then George heard a horrible, rasping cough. He shone the light towards the sound and saw him, Uncle Zeedie, scrabbling blindly through the last of the vampires' tunnel. A great relief swallowed George up...

And then he shone his light beyond, and it spat him back out.

There, in the tunnel, stood the jawless boy. He was filthy, breathing hard, but he was unharmed. His jaw hung slack, those evil little teeth glittering in George's torchlight. A malevolent smile twisted at his eyes, and he walked closer.

"Stop..." George said, but it was a waste of time. The boy was going to kill him, and he felt sick, and oh god, his head, his head...

Somewhere in the dark there was a whispering sound, too faint to understand. Uncle Zeedie heard it too, and turned to look, and so did the boy, because doubt suddenly crept into his eyes. A lantern appeared just behind him, then a lamp, then a tealight. Then a hundred lights, each one held by the hand of a child. The faces of murdered children surrounded the jawless boy on every side, whispering at him with a rapt malevolence.

"*Hth*..." the Kazluk boy said. He sounded afraid. Some of the children smiled, some of them didn't. All looked ready to commit revenge.

Then the ghosts swooped, and the tunnel collapsed.

George clambered up the basement stairs, a terrible fatigue gripping his limbs. The hallway was already thick with dust, and he could barely breathe. He wanted to lie down, but knew that if he did so now, he wouldn't get up again. He made a dash for the front door, and—

"George," Uncle Zeedie gasped. "Wait."

George stopped. Uncle Zeedie was in even worse shape than he was; doubled over, gulping desperately for air. He raised a finger, a sign to listen. In the distance there were footsteps, and a terrifying, screeching roar that filled George with dread.

"We can't outrun them," Uncle Zeedie choked. "We can't go out there, George."

He was right, George knew. Exchanging a frightened look, the two raced up the floating stairs . . . The air grew clearer of dust as they climbed, but any relief George might have felt died as they reached the first floor and continued up the spiral staircase. Where was Lacey? And when the Kazluk got here, what could he and Uncle Zeedie possibly do to stop them? They reached the top of the spiral stairs, hurried into Uncle Zeedie's office, and George slid the door shut behind them. Uncle Zeedie was still gasping for breath, and the tears in his eyes, the look of abject failure in his normally emotionless face, it all underlined just how doomed they were.

"Good boy, George," Uncle Zeedie's voice was hoarse. "I'm sorry. I don't know what we do now."

And downstairs, the back door opened.

Chapter Thirty-Eight

"Uncle Zeedie?" Lacey said.

The figures behind the door of Uncle Zeedie's office were plastered with grime and dirt. But it was her uncle, and standing behind him, her brother. Lacey breathed out, a shuddering breath of nearly-grief.

"Lacey . . ." Uncle Zeedie moaned, "Lacey you should have run—"

"There's no time," Lacey whispered, placing a hand on his shoulder. "I'm going to climb up this ladder. When they follow me you have to push the ladder up and close the hatch behind them."

"We can't leave you up there with those things!" George began angrily, and Lacey grabbed his hands in hers, gripping so hard that he shut up.

"Please trust me," she said.

There was time for no more. Footsteps bounded up the stairs, and without a moment to lose Lacey raced up the ladder, praying that her uncle and brother would be hidden when the Kazluk got up here.

She flew up onto the warm, wooden loft floor. The blinds were still closed, and only when she'd grabbed the clicker from its place on the shelf did Lacey panic. Could these windows even open? She raced to the nearest window, slid behind the blind and ...

A figure launched itself into the loft, followed swiftly by another. The first figure was not used to these surroundings, and crashed into walls, into the fabric, into everything, before whirling around and running back towards the hole in the floor when—

"—STOP," snarled the creature called Rose, holding up one hand.

The creature called Kendra stopped, and stood, breathing hard, ears pricked. A breeze was coming from somewhere, from the windows behind the blinds. The creature called Rose strode towards them, ready to tear them down and devour whatever was hidden behind—

A crashing sound made her whirl around. With surprising force, the steps they had climbed were slammed up into the room, smashing into the creature called Kendra. There was a rapid clicking sound, and the creature called Kendra shrieked with fury, leaping for the hole, but the clicking sound did not end and ...

The hole in the floor was shut. The way they had come in was no longer a way out.

The creature called Rose had not felt fear for a long time. Now she did. She turned back to the window, reached for the blind, and ...

A new sound came from above the window. It was a hum, and

just as she heard the window click shut behind the fabric, just as she heard footsteps running away across the roof, Rose took a step back ... and felt a deeper fear.

Because the blinds were lifting, all by themselves.

And, through the window, the first rays of daylight were peeking over the valley's edge.

Outside on the roof, Lacey ran for the sun racing westwards towards her. A crashing sound came from the loft behind her, and the moment she felt the sunrays cast their cool morning warmth upon her face, she came to a stop. At the sound of another smash, then another, then another, she turned around. What she saw was ... hideous.

It was Kendra. She was literally glitching out, like a pigeon stuck in a classroom, flying from one window to another. The sunlight was speeding across the roof now, and as it began to shine into the loft, it clipped her arm, and crackled, making her jerk away in a sudden inhuman spasm. Far from slowing her down, this made her speed up, and seconds later she clipped the sunlight again, then again, then again, each time the jerk more violent, each time the crackle more pronounced. Soon she was shuddering, no longer running but bathing in sunlight like it was lava. Lacey smelled roasting meat, off meat, tucked her face into the crook of her arm in a gag reflex. By the time she looked up again Kendra was a lick of flame, a sweating joint bouncing off glass and slowly but surely withering.

But that still left Rose.

Lacey heard the tinkling of smashed glass and was snapped from her grim fascination. The sound had come from the far window, the only one that remained shaded from the summer sun, and as Lacey took a step back, mouth curled down in horror, Rose strode out to face her.

There was thirty metres of rooftop, basking in sunlight, between them.

"You... you'll die," was all Lacey could think to say.

Rose looked over her shoulder, at the still-shaded woods behind, at the collapsed scar across the woods. She could make it. She could escape.

Then she turned to face Lacey. And ran.

Her right leg was the first to stumble. She was halfway across the roof to Lacey, but when it buckled it sent her swerving left, a lick of flame vomiting from her flesh. Rose dug in with a snarl, but then her right leg was buckling; her arms, that had just been pumping her speed on, fell limply to her side as her face began to... *melt*, was the only word Lacey could use to describe it. Still Rose snarled, biting at the air, her eyes bursting like grapes. Rose, or what had been Rose, toppled to her knees at last, her entire body shimmering and shaking with the flames that engulfed her. Then, still with those bubbling, broiling eye sockets pointed at her former friend, Rose reached out with a molten stump of a hand...

...and collapsed.

The vampires, the Kazluk. They were all dead.

Chapter Thirty-Nine

They climbed through thick trees for what felt like miles of grey dawn – not night, not day – and exhaustion swamped them like a blanket. George was cold, and tired, and determined not to moan. He'd changed. And then, just when he was about to ask *when* they would get there, because that was only a fair question, he saw...

"Look!" he exclaimed. "A squirrel!"

They all stopped and watched it. It was a rare type, a red squirrel. George hadn't seen a red squirrel before. It scurried across the trees downhill, then stopped, stark still, as it caught sight of these strange humans. Then, as if deciding he wasn't a threat or even an interest, it carried on down the hill, down to where the vampires' territory had once been. A moment later, he heard a strange birdsong, almost like a duck's bill clapping, and glimpsed through the trees a large white shape flying overhead. Soon, the sounds of wildlife grew louder and more frequent, like somebody had just pressed play on an SFX clip.

"They're coming home," George said. "Can you hear them all? They're safe to come home now!"

"Probably not," Uncle Zeedie said. "More likely the creatures leave these woods during the Kazluk's presence, and return during their hibernation. We've probably disrupted their natural cycle. The wildlife population will likely suffer losses, if anything."

"Uncle Zeeds," Lacey chided him at the look on George's face. Uncle Zeedie looked baffled – then pursed his lips.

"Apologies," he said stiffly, and as they continued up the hill Lacey gave George a grin. Still, it was nice to look at the creatures and pretend they were all coming out to thank him.

"We're here," Lacey said, and offered George a hand. Gratefully he took it, and she hoisted him up onto the road. Sunlight bathed them, and the whole world looked different, just like that. George stood there, shivering in its warmth, then turned. Behind him was the shop, *Rose's Stores*, Uncle Zeedie jogging over towards it.

Uncle Zeedie found car keys in the shop's office, and Lacey found the car parked just behind it. They piled in, and George didn't complain even though the car was *freezing*, and Uncle Zeedie spent ages trying to start it . . . before stalling it straight away.

"I don't drive often," he said at last. But the car started on the next attempt, and they began to drive, very slowly, along the road out of here.

"Uncle Zeedie . . ." Lacey said. "I was so horrible to you. I honestly thought you were . . . Well, for what I thought,

I am... so sorry."

Uncle Zeedie looked at her, that weird smirk on his face. "I would have suspected me," he said, and suddenly it wasn't a smirk, it wasn't even weird. It was just his face. Still, Lacey would've like to have explained herself, to explain how it wasn't him, it was all the evidence and... but a wave of fatigue was sweeping over her. She checked her phone. Five per-cent battery, but one bar of—

"The tank is only a quarter full," Zeedie said. "So we really want to hope for signal before—"

"I've got signal."

She went to WhatsApp, and before George could warn her not to, she hit the 'Famalam' group, the one that called him, their mum, and their dad... all at once.

Before she could realise what she'd done, it was too late. Both their mum and dad's faces opened in split screen, looking at first pleased to see them... then craning in, concerned. Like a sketch, their conversation literally happened at once:

*"Hi, Lacey, I'm just out
for my jog—"*

*"Morning, hun, this
is a bit early, isn't it?"*

"What's happened?"

"Wait, are you okay?"

"Zeedie? Where are you guys?"

*"Is that a cut
on your face?"*

"Mum, Dad, we're okay," Lacey said quickly. "We just . . . this horrible thing happened, and we're driving out now, I . . . I . . ."

That's when the tears started to fall. They came out of nowhere, and then they wouldn't stop. Uncle Zeedie awkwardly lifted his hand to pat her on the shoulder, then patted the air around her instead, while her mum and dad kept haranguing her.

"Lacey? Oh, Lacey, what's wrong?"

"Lacey, what's the matter, sweetie?"

"George? George, you look shaken up, what's happened? I knew you shouldn't have gone to that place so far out, and Zeedie – sorry, Zeedie, I'd said this would be too much but—"

"Wait, are you okay?"

"Let's not do this, let's not make this about us."

"I'm not making this about us—"

"Come on, Lacey, you can tell your dad—"

"Oh who's making it about them now? You're such a child, you—"

"That's right, read everything into every goddamned word—"

Lacey was about ready to scream, when her kid brother reached out and tapped the red button.

"George!" Lacey exclaimed, as her mum and dad's arguing faces froze, then the screen went blank. She looked back to him, but George didn't reply. Instead, he looked unhappily at a cobweb in the corner of his window, and shifted grumpily in his seat.

"Eurgh, these seats are so uncomfortable," he moaned, itching his bum left and right. "Can you turn the heater up? I'm really cold. How long till we get something to eat?"

Too tired either to answer George or argue with him, Lacey put away her phone, sat back in her seat, and watched the scenery crawl by. Soon her eyelids began to close, and as they did, the ghost of a smile crossed her face. Uncle Zeedie really was a bad driver, and she knew her brother would complain a lot more before the journey was done.

She was so glad they were here. She was so glad they were okay.

Epilogue

"And we'll landscape the sinkhole – we can turn it into a beautiful pond, can you imagine, darling? Those woods will need taming anyway, we might as well prettify the whole basin."

"Oh lovely, those pokey old changing rooms can be expanded as well. Perhaps a terracotta theme for the veranda, something mildly Aztec for the roofs?"

"Yes, *brilliant* – the swimming pool can be widened, and once we fix the damage to the roof we can start renovating the interiors..."

Yawning, Chris left his parents and walked out through the broken back door. Already he was bored – they'd said it would be a holiday for him all week, but it didn't feel like it. He didn't mind so much, except if he didn't meet anyone else his own age soon he'd go nuts.

With a sigh, he clambered up onto the sunken and malformed earth, taking the hill up towards the thick woods. He was halfway there when he spied something strange. Sticking out of the ground were oddly-trimmed hedges. Chris fancied he could see forms in them – like bunny ears here, and some kind of antler there.

Shrugging it off, he continued up the hill and into the woods.

The hill was steep and arduous, but Chris didn't really mind. There was no danger of getting lost, what with that bizarre churned-up path leading all the way to the house like an earthworm's burrow. It would be pretty awful to get lost here though, he imagined. All those tight-knit trees getting tighter the more you got lost, the already dark land growing darker still. It was cool here, but it'd be better with more paths and...

And then the trees cleared. The ground dropped down quite suddenly here. It was much softer too, thin grasses growing along it like a flower bed already coloured in with a gentle wave of green. This mini-dip punctuated the end of the sinkhole path, and it wasn't mini, it was *huge*... but that wasn't what caught his attention.

What made Chris stop was the hole.

It made no sense, this hole. It was almost vertical, and deep, and there were no fallen trees beside it, nothing to hint at how it came to be here. Chris peered down at it. What was it, about thirty feet deep, something like that? At the very bottom, there was what looked like a pile of clothes and a large papery sack with nothing inside, although it was hard to tell in the gloom. There were deep finger marks up the side of the hole, pressed into the thick clay deeper down. And...

And there was a girl standing behind him.

"Oh my gosh!" Chris said, startled. He turned around

and stared at her. She was filthy, covered in dirt. "Did you . . ." he began, then paused, because it was a ridiculous question. *Did you dig this hole?* Instead, he cleared his throat.

"I'm Chris. Er . . . what's your name?"

And Izzy smiled.

IN THE SAME SERIES:

-About the author-

Frank Cadaver was born in the witching hour, beneath a blood-red moon and under a bad sign. His first words were not fit to print. Now he scratches stories with yellowed fingernails, across the mouldering walls of the abandoned nuclear power station he calls home. If you like what you read, we'll dare you to find out more...